# SOMA
# BLUES

**By Robert Sheckley
from Tom Doherty Associates, Inc.**

*The Alternative Detective*
*Draconian New York*
*Immortality, Inc.*
*Soma Blues*

# SOMA BLUES

## ROBERT SHECKLEY

A TOM DOHERTY ASSOCIATES BOOK
NEW YORK

This is a work of fiction. All the characters and events portrayed in this novel are either fictitious or are used fictitiously.

SOMA BLUES

This book is printed on acid-free paper.

Edited by David G. Hartwell

A Forge Book
Published by Tom Doherty Associates, Inc.
175 Fifth Avenue
New York, NY 10010

Forge® is a registered trademark of Tom Doherty Associates, Inc.

Library of Congress Cataloging-in-Publication Data

Sheckley, Robert.
    Soma blues / Robert Sheckley. —1st. ed.
      p.     cm.
    "A Tom Doherty Associates book."
    ISBN 0-312-86273-3 (hardcover : acid-free paper)
    I. Title.
  PS3569.H392S65   1997
  813'.54—dc20                   96-32449
                                  CIP

First Edition: April 1997

Printed in the United States of America

0 9 8 7 6 5 4 3 2 1

This book is for you, Gail, my wife, my wondrous combination of intellect, feeling, and beauty, my first inspiration and most important reader. How did I ever get so lucky?

# ONE

# PARIS

# 1

It was an easy one-day drive from Paris to Grisons in Switzerland. Hob brought along his friend Hilda. Hilda was a Dutch girl who had become a French citizen, had a job at Rroukes Gallery in Paris, and had command of a number of European languages. Hob hadn't been sure his French would be sufficient in Switzerland, and he had no Schweizerdeutsch, indeed no Deutsch at all. Also, Hilda was a lively and pretty companion of the blond milkmaid variety and seemed a perfect choice to help Hob winkle out the dark and well-kept secrets of an expensive European sanitorium and spa.

He parked his rented Renault in the visitor's lot, and he and Hilda walked to the main reception area. It was an early summer day, cool and bright in the Swiss Alps, the sort of day in which you were glad to be alive even if you weren't in Ibiza.

Hob had a number of ideas about how to get around the no doubt strict sanitorium system. He had decided upon a direct approach first, just to test the defenses and see how formidable they were.

At the main desk Hilda asked to see Mr. Sertoris, as Hob had told her to do. She was told that Mr. Sertoris was not having any visitors. All this was in English, which he could have done himself.

"But this is ridiculous," Hilda said. "We have driven all the way here from Paris at the express request of Mr. Sertoris's daughter. And we are to be sent away without even speaking to him?"

"It's not my fault," the receptionist said. "It is Mr. Sertoris's orders himself."

"How am I to know that?" Hilda asked.

"We have a paper from Mr. Sertoris authorizing this. We can show it to you if you like."

Hilda glanced at Hob. Hob narrowed hs eyes slightly. Interpreting, Hilda said, "It's easy enough to show a paper. But we want to see the man himself."

"Oh, as for that," the receptionist said, "there will be no difficulty."

"I beg your pardon?" Hilda said.

"Mr. Sertoris and others have come to this place as much to escape from relatives as for any other reason. It is for their own peace of mind that they refuse to visit with their kin, and we respect that wish. But as for *seeing*—" She glanced at her watch. "Yes. Come with me."

Hob and Hilda followed the receptionist down a hallway, up a flight of stairs, and down a very broad corridor to a glassed-in area.

"There he is," the receptionist said.

Looking through the glass, Hob could see a fair-sized indoor skating rink. There were several dozen older people skating on the ice. Prominent among them was a tall, skinny old man in warm-up pants and maroon sweatshirt. Hob didn't even have to look at his photographs to know that this was Mr. Sertoris.

"As long as our patients are ambulatory," the receptionist said, "the ice skating is part of their regular routine. And we make the viewing of them available to whoever asks. That way, there are no suspicions. You'd be surprised what some people think when they're told they can't see their parents."

"I can imagine," Hob said. "Mr. Sertoris looks well."

"Oh, yes," the attendant said. "He is in amazing health. We expect him to go on for years and years."

And so, when he returned to Paris, Hob had to file a negative report for Thomas Fleury, who had so been looking forward to inheriting Uncle Sertoris's money and thus finally able to move from his small luxury finca in San Juan, Ibiza, to a big luxury finca in Santa Gertrudis—he had one all picked out, a place that would be large enough for all his guests and his four Afghan hounds. The Alternative Detective Agency's report was the end of Fleury's dream. Also the end of Hob's stipend. And it came just before the beginning of a new case.

# 2

AFTER THE SERTORIS affair, Hob decided to hang around Paris for a while and see if anything turned up. He took advantage of a long-standing invitation to bunk for a few days with Marielle Lefleur, a senior editor at Editions Charlemagne. The few days stretched to a few weeks, money ran out as it always did, and everyone's patience began to wear thin.

Hob knew it was not going to be one of his better nights when Marielle came back from the office more tired than usual. She dropped her briefcase filled with manuscripts and page proofs onto one of the chairs, walked over to the window—without saying a word to Hob—and looked out.

The apartment was on the fifteenth floor of the Salles des Armes Apartotel, the new structure on the boulevard. General LeClerc just above boulevard Montparnasse. From the terrace you got a wonderful view of the switching yards of the Montparnasse station. The sky was a fish-belly white, lit up coldly by the glow of Paris's lights. The apartment itself was narrow, but it had a lot of rooms. On the walls were photographs of relatives, of Marielle's children, presently on holiday in Brittany. There was a picture of Marielle herself, standing with Simone de Beauvoir. That had been taken four years ago when Editions Charlemagne had published de Beauvoir's book about her journeys around America with the tow-headed young Italian fencer about whom she wrote so movingly in *Auprès de ma Blonde.*

"So what is it this time?" Hob asked.

"I've asked a few people over," Marielle said. She was smoking again, her harsh Gitanes. She chain-smoked them, all day and sometimes half the night. Hob, a smoker himself, had grown to hate their smell, the harsh black tobacco mingled with sour red wine that was Marielle's characteristic odor.

"Christ, who in hell is it this time?" Hob asked.

She rattled off a few names. All publishing people, all a bunch of sluts as far as Hob, with his old-fashioned sexist vocabulary, was concerned.

"I told them you'd make your famous chili," she said.

"Oh, no," Hob said. "I'm not making any chili. Never again. The butchers grind the meat too fine. It always comes out chili pâté."

"You must explain to them," Marielle said. "You can speak French; tell them."

"My French is deserting me."

"That is because you never speak it. Why don't you speak to me in French?"

"I can't make my mouth do those contortions," Hob said.

She looked at him reproachfully. "What is the matter with you? You are never fun anymore."

It was true, Hob thought. But how was he supposed to have fun? What was he doing living in this apartment with this woman? He had his own place, the dreary little apartment on the boulevard Massena that he shared with Patrick, his Irish flute-player friend from Ibiza. Recently Patrick had returned from his trip to Pau with Anne-Laure, the Frenchwoman he was seeing, and had come to an arrangement with her. He would move into her small rent-controlled apartment near the avenue d'Ivry as soon as her son returned to the Institute of Musical Studies in Rome. Meanwhile, with Hob's permission, he had agreed to put up her relatives in the Massena flat so they could take a holiday in Paris. And so Hob had moved in with Marielle.

Proximity had been a bad idea. He didn't like Marielle. Had he ever liked her? Yes, at one time. But that was before he'd lived with her. Why did she insist on leaving the cheeses out? She said that refrigeration spoiled their taste. Cheeses should remain at room temperature. To rot in peace, Hob said. The first of their big fights had been over cheese. Strange what people will find to argue about. There were so many other things to torture yourself over. Why don't you love me? was always a good one—and applicable in this case to both of them. But what they fought about was the cheese.

There were plenty of other things wrong, too, but the biggest of them was no fault of Marielle's. Hob was broke. He was, not to put too fine a point on it, doing exactly what Jean-Claude did for a living. He was living off a woman.

It was true that he received no actual cash money from her. But he got his board, and he got to eat whatever was around. They both lived with the pretense that Hob was waiting for a check from America. It wasn't entirely a lie, sometimes checks did come to Paris from America, and sometimes they were even sent to Hob. But not often and not frequently and of late not at all.

Still, the pretense was important. Marielle was short and squat. She wore the voluminous dark Parisian clothes of a middle-aged woman. They contrived to make her look even squatter than she was. Naked, she had a passable body. Not that Hob cared anymore.

And then the telephone rang. Marielle answered it. "It's for you," she said to Hob.

# 3

"HOB? IT IS Fauchon."

"Hi, Inspector. What can I do for you?"

"If you are not too busy at the moment," Fauchon said in his precise way, "I would appreciate your coming down here. Is now convenient?"

"Just as you'd like," Hob said.

"It is just past 2100 hours. Come to the square outside of Métro Sainte-Gabrielle at 2200 hours. Yes?"

"Sure. What's it about?"

"Somebody you might be able to identify for us." Fauchon cleared his throat and hung up.

The message from Inspector Fauchon had been precise, though on closer examination its vagueness showed through: meet me at Métro Sainte-Gabrielle at 2200 hours. Very good. But first of all, where was that particular stop on the Paris underground system? Hob had to consult his map, and then he found it, on the extreme eastern edge of Paris, just beyond the city limits, in Bagnolet. But why at 2200 hours? Policemen like to be precise. But 2200 hours, which translated to ten o'clock at night, was damned inconvenient.

His French had deteriorated as the relationship with Marielle fell apart. Forgetting his French was a sort of unconscious and ineffectual revenge on his part, he figured because he enjoyed nothing quite so much as a spot of self-analysis combined with a bit of self-pity.

But Marielle expected him to be there, and Hob was in no mood for one of her rages, which were of several varieties: cold rage, indifference, haughty politeness, and scathing irony, none of which he liked. On the other hand, though he didn't much care to admit it to himself, Fauchon had a hold over him. Hob's recent activities in Paris on behalf of his Alternative Detective Agency had involved one or two illegalities. If Fauchon wanted, he could revoke Hob's provisional license to practice as an investigator in Paris within certain carefully prescribed limits. It was a little bit like being licensed to be a painter, but only of Impressionist works and never under any circumstances to use the color orange.

Fauchon had called upon him before for the sort of help that a rundown American with a rapid, shambling gait and an acquaintanceship with half the *goniffs* of the Paris demimonde could be expected to have. What would happen if he didn't show up for this rendezvous? Probably nothing. Maybe, everything. Fauchon could revoke his *carte d'identité*. Fauchon, like any senior police official, had his contacts with Immigration and the other branches of government. But maybe it would be better to call his bluff, what the hell, and put an end to this bloody suspense.

As for Marielle, let her rage. Just because he slept with her didn't mean he had to cook the goddamned chili for her friends.

And anyhow, it was expensive to cook chili, especially accompanied by tamales and enchiladas and tacos. It was expensive because unless you started from scratch with beans and tomatoes and garlic, the only way to have your own Mexican food at home in Paris was by buying it in cans at exorbitant markups in fancy food stores that seemed to think canned chili a delicacy and charged accordingly.

It took him almost an hour to get to Sainte-Gabrielle. He had decided that this was the end, once and for all, he'd better have it out with Fauchon. Besides, he was curious about why Fauchon had chosen this strange hour and out of the way place for their rendezvous. It wasn't like Fauchon to be whimsical while on duty.

The Métro stop at Sainte-Gabrielle was deserted. Hob left his second-class car and walked down the long tiled corridor with the wall ads for Gauloises and Printemps and vacations in "Sunny Martinique." A bum was sleeping on one of the long wooden benches that lined the corridor. He was ragged in a comic way, with a bristly red stubble over his wine-reddened face. He mumbled something as Hob passed, but Hob couldn't quite catch it and probably couldn't have translated it if he had. Does a mumble in an incomprehensible language count as an omen? Hob went through the pneumatic doors and up the long, grimy stairs to the street.

He had never been in this part of Paris before. The buildings were shabby and rundown. There was a low moon, partially veiled by a thin fog through which the streetlamps shown with diffused amber brilliance. The streets were wide, and the few men who passed looked North African—small men in shapeless gray and brown clothing. The streets were arranged in the familiar French *étoile* fashion: four or five roads spoking around a central hub. Across the street and a few doors up was a police van. Two police motorcycles, their red and blue lights still flashing, were parked beside it. Fauchon would be over there, no doubt. Hob started across, then stopped to let an ambulance slide in beside the motorcycles.

A policeman came up, and Hob told him that Fauchon had sent for him.

"Wait just a moment," the policeman said. "He is just finishing an interrogation."

"What's it about?" Hob asked.

"The Inspector will tell you what he wishes."

Fauchon was lucky enough to have an eyewitness account of the murder at Métro Sainte-Gabrielle. Two witnesses, in fact: old Benet, the retired ringmaster from the Lémieux Circus, and Fabiola, the India Rubber girl. Not actually a girl, of course; Fabiola was in her forties. But her long, pale face was unwrinkled, and her hair was tied back in a long braided pigtail. In repose, she gave an appearance of boneless and oddly inhuman grace. She was extremely thin, probably no more than a hundred pounds, yet her movements were so supple that even in so simple a thing as lighting a cigarette she reminded Fauchon of a snake. Her straight black hair had an oily sheen to it and was tied with a bit of colored wool. She was blue eyed, with a tiny rosebud mouth and a pointed chin. She wore a small diamond on the third finger of her right hand—Benet's gift, no doubt, though where the old man had found the money for it was beyond conjecture. The Lémieux Circus wasn't noted for largesse toward its retired members. Benet was a big man, getting on toward his seventies. His thin gray hair showed traces of former dyeing. It was combed in streaks that showed his freckled pink skull. He wore a black-and-white check suit, one step above a circus clown's, a little tight on him now that he was growing a paunch. He had fierce, hooded eyes and a small gray mustache that he brushed with the back of his hand.

Benet had come out of the Métro Sainte-Gabrielle at approximately nine-thirty that evening. Fabiola had been with him. It was a Thursday, the day he went to Samaritaine to take part with the other circus old-timers in their circus festivity for the children of Paris in honor of Saint Edouard, the patron saint of circuses. It had been a chilly day for June, quite unseasonable, and he had worn his English tweed overcoat and Fabiola was wearing her sealskin jacket, the sole possession she had brought from Riga with her in 1957, when she made her escape to Stavanger in Sweden.

"I didn't notice anything wrong at first, Inspector," Benet said. "You don't expect to run across a murder at Sainte-Gabrielle. It is a poor district, but quite a safe one. Good working-class people. Some retirees, like ourselves. Did you ever see us perform, Inspector?"

"I did not have that pleasure," Fauchon said.

"Well, never mind. I was good enough, if I say so myself. But Fabiola, she was sensational. The grace of a temple odalisque."

"What was the first thing you noticed?" Fauchon asked.

"Well, the first thing was people shouting. They didn't sound frightened, not particularly. You know how quickly an argument can boil up in the streets. That's what I thought it was."

"Tell him about the horse," Fabiola said. Her voice was light, soft, breathy.

"It plays no part," Benet said, patting her hand. "You see, Inspector, there were the people shouting, and then some people were running, and then a horse came running down the street. Naturally we thought the horse was somehow a part of whatever was going on. It was only later we learned that Scharnapp, the old-clothes dealer who lives in the rue Sainte-Gabrielle and stables his horse in the little cul-de-sac just behind—Fourgerelles, it is called—well, sir, Scharnapp had unhitched his horse and was preparing to lead it into the stables to rub it down, give it food, water, talk to it—I used to come with him sometimes, because there's something comforting about a horse, especially for a man like myself who has been a ringmaster and lived around animals all his life. But now the horse was running, you see, wild-eyed with fear because the car had grazed its side when it came around the corner on two wheels, tossing poor Scharnapp against the stone-fronted house when its right-side fender caught him in the middle of his back. But before that, although I didn't see it, the car had cut through the crowd, knocking down Mme. Sauvier who owns the dress shop down the block and two other people I didn't know. I am glad to hear they will live, Inspector. It was a classical nightmare—the people shouting, three of them down when the car smashed through them in pursuit of the man with the straw hat. The hat had a shiny green band. Funny what the eye sees, even at a moment like that. I saw his face clearly enough, and I had seen him once or twice before. But I didn't know his name. He was a stranger to the district, probably a foreigner."

Fabiola said, "The car was after him, you see. First the one car, the Peugeot, and then the other, the little German one. What was it, André?"

"A Porsche," Benet said. "A nine-eleven. They are not difficult to spot. And they corner like the devil, eh? I suppose it adds a certain frisson, to be killed by a car like that."

"The Porsche didn't kill him," Fabiola said.

"Not for lack of trying. But you're right, it didn't kill him. The man had been leaving the Café Argent in the Square Sainte-Gabrielle when the cars came for him. He dived for the gutter. He must have hurt his shoulder, landing like that on the cobblestones, but at least he saved his life. For the moment, anyway. I don't suppose he'd had time to think about the other car."

"It came from the other direction," Fabiola said. "It was a big car."

"A Mercedes three-fifty, I believe," Benet said. The driver must have seen him go under the car. So he put the Mercedes right into the parked car. He must have been going forty kilometers an hour and he went into it head on. I don't remember what make the parked car was—perhaps an Opel. The collision rocked it right up onto the curb. It uncovered the man in the straw hat like taking off a turtle's carapace. Only he didn't have on his straw hat any longer. It had come off when he dived under the car."

"He had blond hair," Fabiola said. "He wore a leather jacket. It looked expensive."

"And he lay there for a moment, blinking. Then he must have seen the first car, the Porsche, come around, because he scrambled to his feet and began to run, like the other people. I suppose there were a dozen out there. Some had come out of the café to see what the trouble was. They found themselves being chased by these two cars. Then, I don't remember how, the cars were in the Square Sainte-Gabrielle."

"They had mounted the curb following the blond man," Fabiola said.

"You know the square, Inspector? The café in the middle with the newspaper kiosk beside it? Cars circle around it, and in the square itself there are a few plane trees and some benches. There's also a bus shelter. The man had run there. And there were other people in the square, too, but the cars ignored them, if not deliberately hitting them can be said to be ignoring them, because they were determined to get the blond man. They were like cowboys, Inspector, trying to cut one longhorn out of the herd. One has seen the movies, one knows. And so they chased him, and he ran from them, dodging around benches. They smashed right through, damaging their cars most horribly. The blond man had not lost his courage. He dodged around, and, when the time seemed right, tried to cut back across the boulevard. And that is when they got him."

Just then a gendarme came over, saluted the inspector and said, "I found this, sir. It was in the man's jacket pocket."

He handed Fauchon a small address book with a sealskin cover.

"That should help," Fauchon said, putting it in his pocket.

"And there's also this," the gendarme said. "The deceased was holding it in his hand."

He handed Fauchon a small green bottle made of what looked like jade.

# 4

"Ah, Hob, good to see you." Fauchon was conservatively dressed as always. His round face expressed gravity. The high eyebrows indicated irony. The narrow upper lip showed reserve; the full lower one, passion, or perhaps gluttony. The small brown eyes were shrewd, and they seemed to glow with a light of their own. He said, "I wonder if you can identify a person for me?"

"Why me?"

"Because he is a foreigner, and we believe he lives in Ibiza."

"What made you think that?"

"That he is a foreigner? Because we have his passport. He is English. As for the Ibiza connection, he was carrying a straw basket with IBIZA embroidered on it. And I believe he is wearing a Spanish kerchief knotted around his neck. Also a Spanish shirt."

"Only about a million people pass through Ibiza a year," Hob said.

"Perhaps he is a resident, like you."

"There must be thousands of year-round residents, most of whom I haven't had the pleasure of meeting. Still, I'll take a look if you want me to."

"I would be much obliged."

"What is it, a traffic accident?" Hob had just caught sight of the hastily erected police barricade. "Unless you have some important reason, I don't think I want to see this. I'm supposed to cook chili tonight, and if I'm right about what's in that car, it's going to kill my appetite."

"Really, Hob," Fauchon said in his precise, idiomatic, and utterly foreign English, "for a private detective you have little taste for blood."

"It may seem strange to you," Hob said, "but even an American private detective doesn't go out of his way to wade in gore."

"Gore," Fauchon said. "Good word. Dickensian? Never mind. Come with me, Hob. This is necessary."

The body had been carried to the sidewalk and a big piece of green canvas thrown over it. Two policemen were standing nearby, their truncheons tucked into side pouches. It had just begun to rain. Drops of moisture beaded the canvas. There was a smell of diesel and gasoline in the air. The mist and light rain were growing heavier. Fauchon rocked back on his heels. He bent down over the tarp and with an economical gesture pulled the tarp halfway down.

The body was that of a blond-haired man in his late thirties or early forties. He wore a white shirt, tieless, the front heavily coated in blood and grime. His slacks were fawn, and he had on white moccasins. He wore a heavy gold chain around his neck. Hob bent to look at the chain. It terminated in a gold coin, its top pierced to allow the chain to pass through. On the coin was a bas relief of two crouched leopards. At last he looked at the face. It had been battered but was still recognizable.

# 5

FAUCHON'S SMALL CRAMPED office was in a stone-fronted building that looked like a bank, occupying most of the block between rue d'Anfer and avenue Kléber. Within its tall bronze-fitted glass doors, protected from the rain, a few policemen were standing around smoking. Most of the Paris night patrols worked out of the old station near the Chambre des Députés. Fauchon's section wasn't interested in the nightly toll of street crimes—the muggings, beatings, wife and husband slayings; all these they left to the gendarmes. Their section was after bigger game. Anything that might have international implications found its way to the Sûreté. A lot of the cases were then reassigned to the appropriate departments. Fauchon and his people did not ordinarily respond to traffic accidents, especially traffic accidents in a far-out sector like Sainte-Gabrielle.

Hob slouched along beside and slightly behind the inspector, a head taller—or half a head because he stooped. They went down the wide central corridor, past offices on either side, only a few of which were lighted. An occasional shirtsleeved figure in an office looked up and waved. Fauchon didn't wave back; his acknowledgment was a grunt. They reached the elevator, a small affair like a closet, to one side of the splendid marble double stairway. Fauchon had long complained about that elevator, which was much too small and much too slow. The Works Ministry claimed they could not install a larger elevator without removing two, perhaps three of the marble pillars that adorned the ground floor. Since the building had been declared a National Treasure, the pillars had to stay exactly where they were.

Fauchon didn't say anything on the ride to the third floor. He was humming and rocking on his heels, his gaze fixed on an upper corner of the elevator as if he expected to see a malefactor appear there—ectoplasmically, as it were. They got out of the elevator on the third floor and turned left, Hob leading now because he had been here before and knew the way. Only a single light glowed at the end of the hall. Fauchon's office was at the end of the hall on the left. He hadn't bothered to lock it. A green-shaded lamp shone over his desk. Fauchon dropped his hat on a hatrack beside his umbrella, sat down behind his desk, and motioned Hob to take a seat.

"Haven't seen you for a while, Hob," Fauchon said. "How is the detective agency going?"

Hob knew, and Fauchon knew that he knew, more about the workings or lack of them of the Alternative Detective Agency than any of its employees, including its owner and chief operative, Hob Draconian.

"The agency is fine, I'm fine, everyone is fine," Hob said. "Now, can we get to it?"

"Get to what?" Fauchon asked, his face all innocence.

"Damn it," Hob said, "stop playing with me, Emile. You brought me out to Sainte-Gabrielle, and you asked me to return here with you. Now, please tell me what in hell you want and let me get home."

"Belligerent, aren't we?" Fauchon said. "Are you that eager to return to Marielle?"

"Not really," Hob said. "Tonight I was supposed to cook my famous chili for an assortment of publishing people."

"Then Marielle is expecting you? Tell her you were detained on police business. That should save you from a row."

"You show little insight into Marielle's character," Hob said, "if you think a legitimate excuse will suffice."

"I could have warned you about that woman," Fauchon said.

"Well, why in hell didn't you?"

"Stop being childish," Fauchon said. "What I dislike about

you, Hob, is that you have no small talk. Don't you ever read detective novels? The cop and the private detective talk about all sorts of things. Insinuations are always made by the policeman before he gets down to cases."

"I have no time to read detective novels," Hob said. "I'm too busy detecting."

"And in your spare time?"

"I read Proust."

"Who was that fellow under the tarpaulin?"

"Stanley Bower."

Fauchon looked annoyed. "You really are poor at this, Hob. You are supposed to say that you never saw him before, and I point out that your eyes widened when you looked at him, and then you admit that you might possibly have seen him once or twice, but couldn't claim to actually *know* him, and so on and so on until I get you to admit that he was in fact your long-missing brother."

"Inspector Fauchon, please be serious. Or if you can't, at least take me out and buy me a decent dinner."

"Marielle does not provide?"

"Our arrangement is that we split all costs. Unfortunately, I have no money."

"What about the famous check from America?"

"It still has not arrived."

Fauchon clucked in mock sympathy. "So Marielle pays for you both?"

"That would be against her principles. It would mean that she was keeping a younger man. No, Marielle buys food for one and assumes that I eat out on my own."

"What do you do?"

"I wait until she's gone to sleep. Then I eat what's left over. Fourth-day lamb or veal roast with the fat nicely congealed around it is always a treat. Stale cheese with green mold for dessert."

"My dear fellow, you have my sympathy. Women's ability to deal out humiliation is only succeeded by man's ability to take it."

"Who said that, La Rochefoucauld?"

"My father, as a matter of fact. He had some great stories about the Ouled-Naïl dancing girls who used to come to his command post at Sidi bel Abbès."

"I'd love to hear it," Hob said. "Preferably over a glass of white wine at Au Pied du Cochon."

"Stanley Bower, I believe you said?"

"Yes, his name popped into my head as soon as I saw him. Pity I can't remember anything else about him."

"Where did you meet him?"

"Blank," Hob said, tapping his head. "They say that hunger makes a man forgetful."

"Hob," Fauchon said, his voice making the transition nicely from jesting to menacing, "do not toy with me."

"Is that a line from one of your detective novels?" Hob asked. "Of course I'm going to toy with you. I'm hungry, and I don't want to go back to Montparnasse and make chili. How the hell can you French think chili is a gourmet dish?"

"It is our special gift," Fauchon said, "to equate the exotic with the desirable."

"Oh, God," Hob said, lowering his head into his hands.

"You're so pathetic," Fauchon said, "I find it difficult to be cross with you. Come along then. Perhaps a plate of pâté will refresh your memory."

"Follow it up with maigret of duck," Hob said, "and I'll tell you what they did with Judge Crater."

"*Comment?*" Fauchon said, choosing that moment to become French again.

They didn't go to Au Pied du Cochon. Instead they went to the Brasserie Lipp, because Fauchon was in a mood for *choucroute garnie.* The Lipp was one of the famous old restaurants on the boulevard Saint-Germain, across the street from Deux Magots. It was a palace of tinted mirrors and amber lights, chandeliers, tuxedoed waiters, and stylish people, who were becoming more and more difficult to tell from the people merely trying to be stylish. There were the inevitable German tourists, of course, and the inevitable British tourists, and the many other tourists who were also becoming inevitable, notably the Japanese. Hob also ordered the *choucroute*. It was large, spicy and filling, and the best the Lipp had to offer. Where the French ever got their passion for sauerkraut and knockwurst was beyond him. These were things the guide books never told you.

Fauchon ordered a white Bordeaux. Hob thanked God for France, where even police interrogations are conducted over a glass of wine.

"Now," Fauchon said, "about this fellow Stanley Bower."

"Who?" asked Hob.

"The person you identified."

"Did I? You know, Emile, I just might have made all that up. In order to get to the Lipp, you know."

"Hob, that is not funny."

"I thought you wanted me to be more evasive and conversational, like your private detectives in books. Aside from those circus people, did anyone else see what went on?"

"We have no eyewitnesses. Of course we interrogated the people at the Café Argent, where this Stanley Bower was just before his murder. We talked to the proprieter, who served them."

"Them?"

"Bower was talking with some fellow shortly before his murder."

"What fellow? What did he look like?"

"He was sitting in the shadow. The proprietor did not get a good look at him. Just a man. He left. Bower left shortly after him, and that's when the cars arrived."

"Nothing else about the other man? Color of hair? Height?"

"He was sitting. He wore a hat. The proprietor couldn't even give us a description of the hat."

"That's great," Hob said. "And for this I'm missing my party."

"What time are your guests due?" Fauchon said.

"Beg pardon?"

"The guests of Marielle for whom you are to cook the chili."

"They're probably arriving just now," Hob said, expertly wrapping a soggy mass of wine-flavored sauerkraut around a bit of rosy knockwurst and popping it into his mouth, following it up with a piece of crusty baguette and a sip of wine.

"Start telling me something," Fauchon said, "or I will summon a gendarme to escort you home. There is still time for you to play host."

"You'd actually do that, wouldn't you?"

"The cruelties of the French police are beyond the comprehension of the Anglo Saxons," Fauchon said with a little smile of satisfaction. He put his napkin on the table and started to get up.

Hob reached out and touched his arm. Fauchon sat down again.

"You're pretty good at making jokes, but you don't take one worth a damn."

"Tell me about Bower."

"English. About forty years old. A nodding acquaintance. Met him in Ibiza a couple of years ago. He knew somebody. House guest. Let me think a moment. Yes, he was staying with Elliot Turner, the actor."

"You know Turner?" Fauchon said.

"Yes. Why?"

"I recently attended an Elliot Turner film retrospective at the Ciné Montparnasse Study Center. Is he as nasty as the parts he portrayed?"

"Oh, much worse."

"They say he is quite a ladies' man."

"They lie. He is a flaming homosexual."

"Indeed? In his movies he is always lusting after somebody else's woman."

"In real life, he was always lusting after somebody else's boy."

"And Stanley Bower was a friend of his?"

"I suppose so. As I said, Bower was staying at Turner's finca in San Jose. His house guest. I never saw them together much, but I imagine either they were friends or Bower was blackmailing Turner."

"Did you learn what Bower did for a living?"

"He didn't seem to do much of anything. I believe there was family money. That's what Bower hinted at, anyhow."

"Hinted?"

"I call it that. Bower liked to buy a round a drinks at El Caballo Negro and brag about his family connections and how his grandfather had been the best friend of Edward the Seventh. Or maybe it was another Edward. That's how he talked to the Americans. But when any English were present, he didn't have much to say about all that. It was impossible to tell whether he was trying to put one over on us or indulging in that British sense of humor that becomes so sly that even it's possessor can't tell who he's sending up."

"Did you know Stanley Bower was a drug dealer?" Fauchon asked.

Hob shook his head. "Explains why you're so interested in this case, though. Are you sure of your information?"

"A small bottle of the drug he was selling was found on his body. It's a new drug. It turned up in New York recently. Have you ever heard of soma?"

"That's a new one on me," Hob said.

"On a lot of people. It's something we might start seeing around, however. Which is why I'd like to get on it before it gets started. Did you see Bower again after his stay in Ibiza?"

"Nope."

"Not even during your visits to London?"

"I told you, no. I didn't like the man. He was one of those haughty types with a loud braying laugh. Pure Wodehouse. I didn't take to him at all."

"But no doubt others found him an amusing fellow?"

"No accounting for some tastes."

"What did Nigel Wheaton think of him, for example?"

"Why don't you ask him? And anyhow, what does it matter? You're not accusing Nigel of supplying Stanley with a new drug and then killing him, are you?"

Fauchon acted as if he hadn't heard Hob's questions. His gaze was vague, far away, taking in the brilliantly lit interior of the Lipp. It was one of his most annoying mannerisms, as far as Hob was concerned, this sudden switch of attention when a point of some importance had finally been reached. Hob felt that he did it by careful design, one of the many faces of Emile Fauchon, all of them carefully devised, none of them the real man, the man within. Who was the real Fauchon? Was there one?

"What has Nigel been up to lately?" Fauchon asked. "I haven't seen him around."

Hob stared at Fauchon bitterly. "This, I believe, is my chance to betray one of my best friends in return for the sumptuous feast you have given me here at this palace of German sauerkraut and French pretension. To act *le stool pigeon,* as your detective novels doubtless call it. And of course I'm happy to oblige. Nigel's been up to the usual thing: a dope deal in Hong Kong, a bank heist in Valparaiso. I believe he also was responsible for last month's political assassination in Montpelier. You know Nigel—he's enterprising, always likes to keep busy."

"Your sarcasm is broadhanded," Fauchon said, "but appreciated nonetheless."

"Thank you. Anything to keep the conversation going."

"Would you care for a drink before we get any deeper into this? And an espresso. Perhaps a double espresso."

"Now you're sounding like Marley's ghost," Hob said.

Fauchon considered it. "Yes, that's apt. I've shown you Christmas Past in the cadaver of your late friend Stanley Bower."

"And who will I meet as Christmas Future?"

"Waiter!" Fauchon called out, halting the balding stoop-shouldered little man in his tracks. "Two cognacs, and two double espressos. And the bill."

"No bill, Inspector. Courtesy of the management."

"Thank the management for me," Fauchon said, "and tell them I'll be arranging for an especially tough health inspector to call on them soon in repayment for their clumsy attempt to bribe me."

"Inspector! It was meant only as a courtesy! I assure you. . . . Inspector, if I tell them that, they'll fire me!"

"Then just bring me the order," Fauchon said. "And the bill."

Relieved, the little waiter scurried away.

Hob said, "Portrait of the incorruptible Emile Fauchon sternly turning down a free meal. Wonderful. I applaud. Now tell me about Christmas Future."

"Very soon," Fauchon said, "I will show it to you. Hob, I expect your help on this matter. In fact, I insist on it. Find out about this Stanley Bower for me. Who might have wanted him dead. The thing appears to have been set up with some care. Find out about this soma."

"Sure. And what are you going to do for me?"

"I will neglect to revoke your license to practice your worthess trade in Paris, as my superintendent has been hinting that I should do. I'm serious about this, Hob. You have contacts in Ibiza. You can find out what is needed to know. Meanwhile, would you like to telephone Marielle and tell her you're being detained?"

"To hell with that," Hob said. "Let her sweat."

"You're a hard man, Hob Draconian," Fauchon said, but he was smiling.

# 6

THE NEXT MORNING, just after Fauchon had gotten through notifying Bower's next of kin, a brother in England, there was a call for him from the New York police. It was a Lieutenant Gherig, a man Fauchon had spoken with several times. The two men were cooperating on international drug smuggling, bypassing the DEA, of which they had a none-too-good opinion, and exchanging information in an attempt to get a handle on an elusive business.

After the usual civilities, Gherig said, "Reason I called, Fauchon, I've come onto a curious case, and I was wondering if you had anything similar. At first I thought it was opium. . . ."

If you want opium in New York, Chinatown is still the place to go. Back in the 1800s, the Chinese fought two wars with the English to keep opium out of their country. The English were persistent: All those poppy fields in India needed markets. And the man-in-the-street Chinaman loved the drug. First Canton was the capital of the export trade, then Shanghai, then Hong Kong. But times changed by the 1970s. Why go through all that hassle with opium—lighting the pipe, taking a hit or two, then cleaning the pipe and starting all over again—when you could get the effect multifold concentrated in heroin? Heroin could be made anywhere, and its market was vastly wider than that of opium. Then cocaine had its vogue, and the days of natural substances seemed over. Chinatowns all over the world provided the main markets in the twentieth century. And for other exotic natural substances. Thus it was no surprise to Lieutenant Gherig that an unidentified man had been found dead of an overdose in one of those dens that sprang up as fast as you knock them down in the vicinity of Chatham Square

"But this guy's no opium user," the sergeant in charge of the detail told Gherig as they stood on East Broadway and Clinton, their faces turning red and blue in the flashing police car lights.

"How do you figure?" Gherig asked.

"Take a look at him," the sergeant said. "It ain't pretty, but it's instructive. He's in fifteen A."

Gherig went inside the tenement, climbed up five steps flanked by two overflowing garbage cans filled with rotted oranges and Chinese newspapers. The front door, with its reinforced steel mesh over what had been a window, was unlocked. Gherig went down a long corridor with cracked linoleum beneath, peeling paint above, forty-watt lightbulbs overhead lighting his way. There were a couple of old Chinese women at the foot of the stairs, and they gabbled at him and pointed up the stairs. Gherig mounted the sagging stairs, up one hopeless floor after another, Chinese children with opaque dark eyes staring at him from doors opened on chains, his stomach protesting because it was less than a month since the hernia operation. At times like this the glamour of his profession escaped him entirely. Up another floor—the fourth? Death is no respecter of the hernias of senior lieutenants, to say nothing of their varicose veins. On the fifth floor there was only one Chinese, a man of middle age in a soiled white suit and Panama hat. "Inside there," he said to Gherig, pointing to an open door at the end of the hall.

"Who're you?" Gherig asked.

"I'm Mr. Lee, the landlord's agent. A tenant telephoned me. I got here as fast as I could."

"Where'd you come from?"

"Stuyvesant Town."

"You got here faster than I did from First Precinct." Gherig walked to the door. The white-suited Chinese followed.

"Lieutenant," Lee said. "Could I just have a word with you before you go in?"

Gherig turned. A big, solid man, he seemed to have about twice the bulk of Lee and stood a head taller.

"What do you want, Lee?"

"I just want to tell you," Lee said, "that neither the landlord nor any of the people here have anything to do with this."

"You're getting in your cop-out a little early," Gherig said. "I don't think nobody's accused you of nothing yet."

"Not yet," Lee said, with a sigh. "But you will."

Gherig walked through the doorway of number 15A into somebody's idea of paradise. There was a red-and-blue Turkish rug on the floor. The walls were covered in brocaded wallpaper showing Oriental sages in tall hats crossing a bridge. There were low settees against two walls. A chandelier hung from a hook in the ceiling; it diffused its beam through a faceted crystal, throwing bright moths of light on the walls. Although the room was not large, it contrived to grow in size through the wall-length mirror on a third wall. There were two low tables, highly carved, of glossy walnut. There was a magazine stand beside one of the settees. It contained two recent issues of *Playboy*, thus answering the urgent question, What do you do while taking a new drug?

"Well, this is a real cute place," Gherig said. "How many more you got like it?"

"This is the only one," Mr. Lee said. "But there's no crime to a man furnishing his place as he sees fit, is there?"

"This place belonged to the deceased?"

"He rented it from Mr. Ahmadi, the owner."

"Ahmadi? What's that, Italian?"

"Iranian."

"And he owns a building in Chinatown?"

"Nothing unusual in that," Mr. Lee said. "Foreigners own everything in America these days."

Gherig asked for the spelling and address and wrote the owner's name in his notebook.

"Did you look at the deceased?"

"Yes, I did."

"Was that Mr. Ahmadi?"

"No, sir. Definitely not. He was the leaser."

"You got Mr. Ahmadi's home phone number?"

"Of course. But you won't find him there now. He's off on a business trip."

"To Iran?"

"To Switzerland."

"Give it to me anyway." Gherig wrote it down, then said, "So that leaves you holding the bag."

"Come on, Lieutenant. I'm the agent for the building. No one put me in charge of having anyone killed here."

"The deceased, what is his name?"

"Irito Mutinami."

"Iranian?"

"Japanese."

"What is a Japanese doing living in Chinatown?"

"A lot of people think it is chic to live down here."

Gherig was prowling around the apartment. The place had been gone over already, but there was no harm in checking it out again. In the wastepaper basket he found a square of bright blue cellophane, twisted as if it had been wrapped around something about the size of a golf ball. Was it some kind of chocolate thing? It looked like what they wrap fancy chocolate balls in. He put it in an evidence bag and went on looking.

In one corner there was a fireplace with an artificial fire glowing in it. Gherig reached in and poked at it, felt something smooth and cool, and lifted it out. It was a bottle of a green substance that looked a lot like jade, about four inches high, uncorked and empty. Gherig lifted it to his nose and sniffed. The odor that came from the bottle was musty and sweet, utterly unfamiliar.

"What's this, some sort of Chinese incense?" he asked, holding out the bottle to Lee.

Lee sniffed. His smooth face turned quizzical. "That's a new one on me, Lieutenant. Never smelled anything like that before."

"Is this jade?" Gherig asked him, holding up the bottle.

Lee shrugged. "Beats me. My hobby's baseball. I know a guy I could ask, though."

"I know somebody, too," Gherig said. "How long had"—he referred to his notebook—"Mutinami been living here?"

"Less than a year," Lee said. "I've had him on the books since early February."

"You happen to know what he did for a living?"

"Student. That's what it said on the form."

"What friends did he have staying?"

"I have no idea," Lee said. "It is my job to collect the rents and effect repairs. I do not spy on the tenants."

Lee turned to leave. Gherig grabbed his arm so suddenly that he spun the smaller man around and had to support him to keep him from falling.

"Lee," Gherig said, "I don't want to have to get this out of you piece by piece. Suppose you tell me all about this Mutinami right now and save yourself a night in the can."

"There's nothing you can hold me for," Lee said.

"Don't worry, I'll invent something."

"We Chinese are a law-abiding people. You have no right to do this."

"I'm not going to do anything because you, as a concerned citizen, are going to tell me all about Mutinami and his friends."

"All right, let go of my arm." Lee brushed himself off, took off his Panama hat, reblocked it and put it on again. Gherig fished an evidence bag out of his pocket and put the jadelike bottle into it. Then he crossed his arms and waited until Lee had straightened his tie, and, presumably, his story.

"I don't know anything about Mutinami or his friends. You have to understand how popular Chinatown is with the Japanese. Several other Japanese businessmen have also stayed here. I presume they were Mr. Mutinami's friends. Or maybe they were Mr. Ahmadi's friends. No one tells me anything. Maybe they were helping out on the rent. How should I know? I don't have their names. This isn't a police state. Not yet, anyway."

"No, but we're working on it," Gherig said. "Lighten up, Lee!

This is a murder investigation. Would you feel better if I arrested you and questioned you down at the stationhouse?"

"I said you wouldn't like what you saw here," Lee said. "But I've told you everything I know. May I go now?"

"Leave your name, address, and phone number with the sergeant downstairs. Don't try to leave town without notifying us. Here's my card. I'm Lieutenant Gherig. If you think of anything else, I'd appreciate your calling me."

"Yes," Fauchon said, "we have had a similar occurrence here. Last night. I'll have to await my pathologist's report to be sure. But there was a green bottle similar to the one you described. I'll telephone when I know more."

# 7

In midafternoon there was a caller at Marielle's apartment. Hob answered it. In the doorway stood a tall, blond Englishman.

"Mr. Draconian?"

Hob somewhat cautiously allowed as how he was.

"I'm Timothy Bower. Stanley's brother. That French policeman was good enough to give me your address. He told me you've been assisting him on this case."

Hob invited him in and gave him a place to sit on Marielle's uncomfortable black leather and chrome couch.

"You're a private detective, I understand?"

Hob nodded.

"Did you know Stanley well?"

"I hardly knew him at all. We said hello once or twice at parties in Ibiza. I don't think we ever had a real conversation."

"Hmm, yes," Timothy said. "I don't mean to be rude, but if you hardly knew Stanley, why are you helping the French police in their inquiry?"

"Stanley lived in Ibiza," Hob said. "That's where I live, too, most of the time. And I'm helping because Inspector Fauchon feels diffident about inquiring into the lives of foreigners who don't even live in Paris and would much prefer I did it for him."

"Hmm, yes. I suppose you know that Stanley was homosexual?"

"Yes. That is to say, it was common knowledge in Ibiza, whether it was true or not."

"Oh, it was true all right," Timothy said. "He'd been a flaming little queer since Eton. I'm sorry, I don't mean to be judgmental, but it was a trial to his family."

"How so?" Hob asked.

Timothy smiled condescendingly. "You know something about England, don't you? Still quite a tight little right little island. People know each other. Especially military families. Our own family dates back to the time of Richard the Lionhearted."

"He was queer, too, wasn't he?" Hob asked. "An affair with a fellow named Blondel?"

"Yes, quite. But it's generally not spoken of. What I'm trying to say is that homosexuality is not respectable in England as it seems to have become in the States."

That was the first Hob had heard of that, but he didn't interrupt.

"Well, this is all very interesting," Hob said. "What can I do for you, Mr. Bower?"

Timothy Bower pursed his lips and looked uncomfortable. He had a rather handsome, tanned face, was probably in his early forties, and didn't seem to know what to do with his hands. He finally brought them to rest on the knees of his sharply creased gray-worsted trousers and said, "This is an extremely upsetting thing—one's own brother being murdered."

"Yes," Hob said with scant sympathy. "But better than the other way around, don't you think?"

Bower let that pass. "The French police seem to have no idea who did it. Do you?"

"Not a clue. It's not my concern, anyhow."

"I don't trust the French," Timothy said. "Especially not in a matter concerning the murder of a gay foreigner."

Hob shrugged. He didn't feel very sympathetic.

"Stanley and I were never close," Timothy said. "I'm regular army. You know how the British army is. Among career officers it's like a club. Gays definitely need not apply. Don't get me wrong. I am not myself prejudiced. I wasn't personally ashamed of Stanley, but I'll be frank to tell you I didn't want him around. Not with the sort of friends I've got. Damned good fellows, don't get me wrong, but for them a homosexual man is a joke. And Stanley was not discreet in his behavior. No reason he should be, I suppose. In a perverse sort of way it shows the family training. The pater taught us never to be ashamed. But none of us ever thought we'd have a homosexual in the family."

Don't be ashamed of yourself unless you have something to be ashamed of, was the way Hob read that one.

"Still, there it is. I feel badly about it. I rather liked Stanley, though I detested his way of life. And Stanley was my brother. I don't want to simply see this thing pushed under the rug. I believe it's common knowledge the French police don't bother much with cases like this."

"Don't kid yourself," Hob said. "The French police are damned good, and they don't push any kind of murder under the rug."

"But what can they do? From what Fauchon told me, this doesn't appear to be a case of local gay bashing. Stanley might have been killed by someone from Ibiza. If that's so, whoever it was is back there by now. Don't you agree?"

"It does look like someone set Stanley up."

"It's clear to me this thing probably has international ramifications. But this police inspector, this Fauchon, he's not going to fly down to your island and try to run it down, is he?"

"Of course not," Hob said. "As yet there's no reason to. But you can be sure he'll make enquiries."

"Yes, I suppose he will. And the Spanish police will say we'll look into it, mañana, and if anyone happens to wander into the station house and confesses to it, we'll be happy to take him into custody, as long as it's not siesta time. No, it's simply not good enough. I want more done than that."

"What is it you want done?" Hob asked.

"You're a private detective. I want you to find his killer."

"All right, let's talk about it," Hob said. "First of all, given what little we know now, it might not be possible. Second, if by some stroke of luck I do find out who did it, that doesn't mean I can prove it. What I'm saying is, even if I can find out who killed Stanley, an arrest may not be possible."

"Well, I'm sure you'll do your best," Timothy said. "I believe I understand the position. It may be a forlorn hope. But I feel one should do something."

"All right," Hob said.

Timothy took out his checkbook and a fountain pen and wrote Hob a check for five hundred pounds.

"I'm by no means a wealthy man," Timothy said. "That's what I can afford. There won't be any more. I'm sure you'll do your best on it."

"I'll do what I can," Hob said. "Where shall I send my reports? And do you want them telephoned as well as written?"

"I don't want any reports," Timothy said. Hob could see that Timothy had made up his mind how to handle this probably on the flight over from London. "If and when you've brought his murderer to book, perhaps you'd be good enough to write me care of my club." He gave Hob a card. "I'd appreciate your not putting a return address on the envelope. In my position, one must avoid scandal at all costs."

Hob didn't like it, but he accepted it. One of the jobs of a private detective is to accept money from people who are trying to buy off their guilt at not doing something themselves. But from a detective's point of view, it was a legitimate case.

# 8

THE NEXT DAY, Hob went to the Café Argent in the Square Sainte-Gabrielle. Usually Hob would have taken Nigel, his chief operative, but Nigel was away on some scheme or another in England. With Nigel absent, Hob brought his other Paris operative Jean-Claude, a skinny little fellow in his early thirties, with brilliantined black hair and a hairline mustache. Jean-Claude looked louche, dangerous, and unpleasant, as always. Today he wore his striped Apaches-of-Paris shirt and tight black pants.

When a waiter came over to take their orders, Hob asked to see the proprietor. The proprietor came over, a short, square, balding man presenting a somewhat harrassed bonhomie.

"I was here last night," Hob said. "I am helping the French police in their investigations."

"Yes, m'sieu."

"This is my associate, Jean-Claude."

The proprietor made a slight bow. Jean-Claude gave him the slitted eye.

"We seek to find out more about the man who sat with the deceased."

The proprietor made an expressive gesture with his hands. "As I told the inspector, I served the man myself. I noted nothing about him except what I have already said."

"I realize that," Hob said. "But it occurred to me that it is slightly unusual for the proprieter to take orders when he has waiters."

"Nothing unusual about it," the proprietor said. "Marcel had just gone off duty, so I filled and served the order myself."

"But did Marcel take the order?"

"Of course. He wrote it up and gave me the slip, and then his time was finished, and he took off his apron and left. Young men these days are all for the union rules as long as they are in their favor."

"You didn't mention this to Inspector Fauchon."

"It slipped my mind in the excitement of the moment. Anyhow, what need? I served the order, and I have already stated what I saw—which was nothing."

"Just so. But perhaps you would oblige us by asking Marcel to come to our table for a few questions. He might have seen something that slipped your attention."

The proprietor shrugged, a gesture that said, "That'll be the day!" But he went to his counter and called for a young waiter who was serving on the far side of the square.

Marcel was young, slim, blond, good-looking. Reminded Hob of a young Jean-Pierre Aumont. And yes, damned if the fellow didn't have his hair marcelled. Sometimes life was very strange, indeed.

"Yes, I took the order. But there was nothing amiss. They were talking together quite pleasantly. And as you know, I was not here when the accident took place."

"What were they talking about?" Hob asked.

Marcel pulled himself up to his full height. "I do not eavesdrop on the customers, m'sieu."

Then Jean-Claude stepped in. "Look here, *mon vieux,* I'm not going to dance around the tables with you. You are a waiter, *n'est-ce pas?* That makes you automatically one of the nosy class. I am going to require that you tell me everything you overheard. If not, I am going to come back and talk to you again, and this time I'll bring several friends along. Not friends like my colleague Hob, here, who is a gentleman. Friends who get results. My boy, we'll have you babbling conversations you never even imagined took place. Why not save all of us a lot of trouble and tell us now?"

Hob winced but said nothing. He did not approve of Jean-Claude's methods, which he considered crude in the extreme. But he had to admit that they frequently got results. It was amazing how many people could be intimidated.

"M'sieu does not have to threaten," Marcel said. "I repeat, I am not a snoop. Anyhow, their talk was conducted in English and Spanish: two languages whose meanings I am not privy to."

"You are trying my patience," Jean-Claude said. "You know something, damn it. I can tell by your stupid shifty eyes and the way you are shifting from one foot to another. No more evasions! For the last time, tell us something we can use."

"It isn't much," Marcel said, "but I can tell you about the map."

"Map? What map? The patron didn't mention a map."

"They must have put it away before he came out to serve them."

"Well, what about the map?"

"They were pointing to it and laughing. M'sieu, I truly did not understand their words. But their manner was that of men exchanging reminiscences and pointing to places where this and this happened."

"What kind of map was it?"

"A gas station map. A Spanish one."

"What was it a map of?"

"I did not see. Someplace in Spain, I presume."

"That's very good," Jean-Claude said. "Now you've begun, don't stop now. What else?"

"Nothing else, m'sieu."

"There has to be something else. What did this man look like?"

"He sat well back in the shadow. But I noticed that his face was very tan. He was middle-aged, I would say. And he wore an emerald ring."

"You're sure it was an emerald?"

"It could have been green glass, for all I know," Marcel said. "But it was cut brilliant fashion. That's a lot of work to go to for a piece of glass."

"Was there anything else about his face?"

"Nothing, m'sieu."

"Now put your attention once again to their words. Can you remember anything at all?"

"Just '*à votre santé.*' They said that in French. Toasting each other. That's why I remember it."

"Which one said it?"

"The stranger. The one who was not killed."

"And the other one—the victim—what did he say?"

"He said, 'And the same to you, Señor.' "

"Señor what?"

"I do not know. He made a strange gargling sort of sound. It may have been the Spanish *r*, m'sieu. But what came before it, and what after, I don't know. And that is all, m'sieu, all, all!"

"You have done well," Jean-Claude said, patting the waiter on the cheek. "Better than you expected, eh? Come, Hob, shall we be on our way? There's nothing further to be learned here."

"So what did all that add up to?" Jean-Claude asked after they had left.

"A dark-faced or tanned man. One whose native tongue is presumably not French, but is likely either English or Spanish. And who perhaps has a name which contained a double Spanish *r*."

"Not much," Jean-Claude said.

"But something. Maybe I can find out more on Ibiza."

"Would you like me to accompany you? Jean-Claude asked.

"Nothing would suit me better. But you'd have to pay your own ticket and expenses. The agency is sadly short of funds."

"Then I shall stay here in Paris, the center of the world. I was only trying to help."

"You are too kind," Hob said.

# 9

FAUCHON HAD SHOWN Hob Stanley's address book. "A courtesy to a colleague," he'd said in an ironic voice. The only name that had meant anything to Hob was that of Hervé Vilmorin, a young French ballet dancer who divided his time between Paris and Ibiza. Fauchon had already questioned Hervé, but Hob was working on Stanley's case now on behalf of Timothy Bower, and so decided his own interview would be in order. Besides, Fauchon wouldn't let him see his interview notes.

Hervé agreed reluctantly to see Hob at his apartment on the rue des Pères, which he shared with several other dancers. Hob went there in the late morning. Hervé was young, very slender, and muscular, his light brown hair modeled into a cut similar to that of Nijinsky in *L'Après-midi d'un faune*. He wore tight, well-cut blue jeans that showed off the development of his thighs and a light-blue cashmere sweater with the sleeves pushed up to display his hairless brown arms.

"I've already told Inspector Fauchon everything I know," Hervé said.

Hob shook his head. "Permit me to make a correction. You told Fauchon everything you thought was safe to say. You know me, Hervé. I'm not going to tell on you. Stanley was selling drugs, wasn't he?"

"Not to me," Hervé said. "I don't buy drugs. People give them to me."

"I wasn't accusing you of spending your own money," Hob

said. "But you've got a lot of friends who are users."

"I wouldn't know anything about that," Hervé said.

"Come on, Hervé! You and I have tripped together. At the Johnstone party. You came with Elmyr de Hory, remember?"

Hervé had been trying to look stern. Now he couldn't help a smile coming across his chiseled lips. "That was quite a good evening, wasn't it?"

"Yes, and the California windowpane was pretty good, too. Look, I'm not trying to trap you into anything. I want to know why Stanley got killed. I'm working for his brother. I won't pass on anything you tell me. So tell me, Hervé."

Hervé thought for a few seconds, then decided that Hob was to be trusted.

"He was selling a new drug. Soma, he said it was called. He was quite excited about it. He said it was expensive but absolutely the best trip going. I gave him a few names. You know Paris people. Interested in the newest novelty."

"Did you try any yourself?"

Hervé shook his head. "Stanley and I were going to take some together. Tonight, as a matter of fact." His mouth drooped in sorrow.

"These people he sold it to. Who were they?"

"Hob, you know very well I'm not going to name any names. Not even for you, my dear. Anyhow, none of them could have been involved in Stanley's murder. Wealthy Parisians don't kill their dope dealers. You know that as well as I do."

"Can you at least tell me who he saw last?"

"Oh, Hob, it isn't going to do you any good. And anyhow, I don't know."

"Come on, Hervé. I need a name. I have to start somewhere. Stanley was staying with you just before he got killed, wasn't he?"

"I've already admitted that to Fauchon."

"So you must know who was the last person he saw."

Hervé sighed. "Oh, all right. It was Etienne Vargas, if you must know. You know Etienne, don't you? The tall, delicious Brazilian boy who came to the island a few months ago?"

"I don't know him. Was he going with Stanley?"

"No way, my dear. Etienne is unfortunately straight. He goes with Annabelle. You know Annabelle, don't you?"

"Yes. Slightly. Is she here in Paris?"

"Not to my knowledge. Etienne apparently came without her."

"Where was he staying?"

"Some hotel, I believe. I don't know which."

"Was he alone or with someone?"

"I don't know. He was alone when I saw him. He said he had an appointment with Stanley."

"How did he act?"

Hervé shrugged. "Brazilian. What else?"

"I mean, was he nervous?"

"Not that I noticed."

"He came here to your apartment?"

"Yes. Said he was supposed to meet with Stanley. I told him Stanley had gone out. Asked if I could take a message. He said no, he had a date with Stanley later, but since he was in the neighborhood he thought he'd drop by. And then he left. Hob, you mustn't breathe a word about me telling you this."

"Don't worry. Can you tell me anyone else who might have bought this soma from Stanley?"

"I gave him half a dozen names to call. I don't know if any of them bought from him. Hob, I really don't know."

"What about Etienne? Do you think he might have bought some?"

"He's rich enough to. The Vargas family is very prominent in Rio de Janeiro. His father has a finca on the island, you know, near San Juan. I told you the stuff Stanley had was pricey. But I have no way of knowing who he sold to."

"I don't suppose you know where I could reach Etienne now?"

"Not a clue, my dear. I'd imagine he's gone back to Ibiza."

# TWO

# IBIZA

# 1

HOB LOOKED OUT the window and saw below, through a thin screen of clouds, the island of Ibiza appear suddenly through a cloud break. He was sitting beside a businessman, fattish and obnoxious, who had begun a conversation by telling Hob that he was from Düsseldorf, had come to Paris on business, and, finishing his appointments early, was taking a long weekend on the Spanish island of Ibiza. Had Hob ever been there? Not waiting for an answer he said that he had a friend who lived in a new condominium near Santa Eulalia—Der Sturmkönig, it was called. Had Hob ever heard of the place? It had been mentioned in *European Architecture* magazine as "a piquant potpourri of styles old and new." It had three swimming pools, a Corinthian arch, a bandstand in the shape of a seashell, and three restaurants, one of which had been awarded four pigs in *International Gourmand* magazine. It had its own shops and food stores, and, very important, its own German butcher who made the sausages and the *Schweinefleisch* and the other good meats of the homeland. There followed a brief dissertation on sausages, ending with, "I am very particular about my sausages. Only the Germans know how to make proper sausages. The French sausages look amusing but have too much garlic and otherwise lack character. The English sausages are carelessly put together and made with sawdust, like their politics. Only in Germany, and especially in the Düsseldorf area, is it known how to make sausages."

Hob nodded agreement throughout the speech. It was the

sort of old-fashioned chauvinistic talk that was so difficult to come by these days, the sort of talk that Hob, a collector of extreme nationalistic attitudes, usually liked to hear, because in his mind Europe was a big Disneyland in which each country had its own quaint colors and costumes and customs and its own special products and its own typical people in regional costumes who were always willing to make speeches about themselves. He thought it charming that the Italians had strong nationalistic opinions about pasta and the Scandinavians about akvavit, and so on, right down to the Belgians with their mussels and *pommes frites*. But typically, he disliked himself for having this cynical and superficial view, thought little of himself for being charmed by bogus quaintness, or even the real thing, real quaintness, whatever that is. He knew what he sought was out of touch with current realities. Europe was no longer quaint. It was in deadly earnest. But not for Americans, who, to their peril, couldn't even take the Japanese seriously. Americans didn't go to Europe to get a dose of reality. There was enough of that at home. They went for the local color. And if they couldn't find it, they made it up.

The plane dropped a wing and banked. Ibiza came fully into view, a small island that the jet could overfly in much less than a minute. There was the central spine of mountains, with the valleys on the southern side and the sheer cliffs coming down to the sea on the northern side. There was the pall of smoke over to one side, from the huge garbage pit near Santa Catalina that burned day and night and was the island's leading eyesore. And then the plane was dropping down toward the airfield, and the seat belts sign came on.

At last he was standing on the dusty tarmac, walking to the luggage area. There was a crowd of people behind the barricades, waiting for friends and lovers. Would there be someone waiting for him? Unlikely. It was close to six months since Hob had last been on the island, when he had come for Harry Hamm's wedding.

And then he was out and into a taxi and smelling the smell of the island: thyme and jasmine, oranges and lemons. He went by the low cubic white houses on the road into Ibiza City. In front of him arose the sight of the D'Alt Villa, the old city, a mass of white cubes rising up out of the ground, all odd angles and shapes, a cubist city of the past, like something out of remote Cycladean Greece.

The driver wanted to chat with him in his rudimentary English. Hob didn't want to talk, however. The first moments of the return to the island were precious. He searched the roadside for familiar landmarks. The map of Ibiza was covered with monuments to the peculiar personal history of the place. Here is the spot where Little Tony got busted by the Spanish drug cops. That pile of rocks is where Arlene had her old bar, where Elliot Paul used to come by for a drink, before the Fascists demolished it. Just down the road is where you met Alicia that first golden summer. And here is the dangerous crossroads where, one hilarious night, Sicilian Richard went off the road in his big gangster Citröen, and ploughed into an Ibicenco house, killing the brother and sister who lived there, catching them together in bed, so the story went. Richard never lived to tell of it. The Guardia came and took him to the hospital for a broken arm. He died of causes unknown on his way there.

Hob's first stop was in the village of Santa Eulalia. He had the taxi drop him off at Autos Carlitos where he hired a SEAT 700. He took the little car out on the road to San Carlos, in the hills just beyond the village. He got a lift of the spirits as he passed through San Carlos, noted the half dozen hippies drinking beer and playing a guitar at the wooden tables outside of Anita's bar, went through the sharp curves with Robin Maugham's house on the crest on the left, and turned into the rocky drive that led to his finca, Ca'n Poeta. He found room for his car near the big *algarobo* tree in front of the sheds. The house with its beautiful lines made him feel better at once. It was built according to the golden mean, or golden section, Rafe the Architect had told him. Whatever it was, the house looked good with its two wings separated by the second-floor drying shed that had laundry flapping from it now. He went down three steps to the flagstoned entranceway with its big grape arbor. There was no one home but a small dark-haired girl in a pink bathing suit lying in the hammock reading an Alistair MacLean paperback. Hob had never met her before. She said she was Sally, Shaul's friend—Shaul being one of Hob's friends from Israel—and that everybody had gone to the beach and who was he? Hob explained that he was the owner, and the girl complimented him on his house and his hospitality.

Hob went inside, put his luggage in his second-floor bedroom, and changed into white cotton shorts, a gray three-button T-shirt, and espadrilles. He left again and drove back out to the San Carlos road, going back toward Santa Eulalia, then turned off at Ses Pines and drove inland between almond fields into the Morna valley. Soon he was climbing toward the Sedos des Sequines, the mountainous ridge that ran down the center of the island. The little car negotiated the steep road without too much difficulty. The narrow rutted road changed to a dirt track and climbed into the steep hills. Several times Hob had to negotiate around rock faces beetling into the road. In Ibiza they tended to build around things rather than blast through them. At last he crawled around a final steep hairpin and saw ahead, where the road flattened across the saddle of the hill, the drystone fence that enclosed Harry Hamm's finca.

Hob parked the car in the space cut for it in the prickly cactus patch, alongside Harry's SEAT. He walked around the edge of the stone fence, and then he could see the house, built on the back slope of the hill. It was a small farmhouse, about two hundred years old, with four or five hectares of land surrounding it. The grounds were scrupulously clean, as Ibicenco farms always were, unless they were being farmed by *peninsulares,* as Spaniards from the mainland were called. To one side were the sheds, still half full of *algorobos,* the ever-present carob. Hob could catch its characteristic sickly sweet aroma. It wasn't a smell he much liked, but he associated it with the island, and so it had become dear to him.

The house itself was typical, built of fitted stones that were encased in mud and brush and then cemented and plastered. As was traditional on the island, the size of the largest room was determined by the length of the trunk of white oak available for the ridgepole. Once the ridgepole was in place, right-angled oak limbs were fitted to either side, then brush was piled on top of that and packed with mud. The roof was flat and slanted toward the center to catch rainwater, which was led to gutters and then down to the underground storage tank from which Harry would pump what was needed up to a holding tank on the roof.

Not even the windows had been modernized, although Harry had decided to do that someday. But he held off, appreciating the fact that in the old days the slit windows kept out the winter's cold and provided no easy entry for the Saracen pirates from Algeria and Morrocco who used to ravage the island until late in the 1800s. The North African coast was less than a hundred miles away. The Saracens had been raiding these islands for hundreds of years, and the Ibicencos, far from any central government, had learned to take care of themselves. Every village and every outlying structure was a fortress, or at least a strong point, designed to hold up the invaders until men could be assembled to deal with them. There were no Saracen pirates anymore, only English and German tourists—and these tended to give more than they took. Hob sometimes wondered if the change had been advantageous. Dealing with raiders had developed hardiness and self-reliance in the Ibicencos; dealing with tourists had been aesthetically disastrous, bringing fast-food restaurants and entire Scandinavian, German, and French "villages," newly built self-enclosed tourist centers whose architecture was all the more grotesque since it was a self-conscious attempt to imitate a small village from back home. No American villages so far, but that was sure to come.

There were a few chickens scratching around the front yard at Harry's place. Maria's doing, no doubt. Hob had never believed that a guy like Harry Hamm was cut out to keep chickens. But what could you tell about Harry's Ibicenco wife except that she was beautiful and stately and obviously much too good for Harry, who was an overweight, balding, retired cop from Jersey City, New Jersey, and Hob Draconian's mostly unpaid partner in the Alternative Detective Agency.

Hob kept to the roadside of the stone fence and hailed the house. "Harry! Are you there?" His voice boomed across the yard, amplified by the freak acoustics of the scalloped cliffside nearby. For a moment there was no answer. Then Harry came running out of the house, in khaki work pants and white shirt, wearing the soft rope-soled espadrilles of the island, a big balding man with a paunch.

"Hob! Come in!" Harry swung open the little gate and led Hob through. Now Hob could see Harry's car, a Spanish-built Citröen parked just around the side of the sheds.

"About time you showed up," Harry said. "You talk me into going into this agency with you, and then you split for Paris and leave me here to moulder."

"In Maria's arms," Hob reminded him.

"Well, yeah, that's right." Harry grinned. "As a matter of fact I like it here fine. But it's nice to have a fellow American to talk to from time to time."

"What's the matter with the Ibicencos?"

"You know I get along with them. It's the French and English I don't much care for."

It was Harry's fate that, without being in any way an internationalist, he fit into the native life of Ibiza easily and well. He could have been a born Ibicenco, since he shared most of their prejudices and possessed more than a few of their virtues.

"Everything okay?" Hob asked him.

"Yeah, fine. I've got to see Novarro, though. He asked me to bring you if you happened to show up."

Novarro was a lieutenant in the Guardia Civil, stationed in Ibiza. Hob had known him for years in a formally friendly sort of way.

"What's it about?"

"I had a little trouble couple nights ago. Nothing important. Tell you about it later."

Harry led Hob into the kitchen, which was large and cheerful, with colorful prints by local artists on the white plaster walls. There was a refrigerator and stove, both operating on bottled gas. There was a butane lamp, too, lit, although it was broad daylight, because the kitchen had only one window, a very narrow one. Harry usually didn't like to use the gas lamp because it hissed and gave out a faint but unpleasant odor. He much preferred to fid-

dle with the Aladdin kerosene lamps because he liked the soft
golden light they cast, and he had taken it upon himself to keep
their mantles clean and the wicks trimmed since Maria, with her
islander practicality, saw nothing romantic about kerosene lamps.
Why use them when butane was so much cheaper and simpler?
Why use either, for that matter, when for a couple of hundred dollars they could get an electric line put in from the transformer station on the main road? Harry wouldn't have it. He liked to keep
the finca electricity-less, since that suited his romantic streak.
Maria liked that about him but found it difficult to explain to her
sisters, to say nothing of the various aunts and uncles and cousins
of her large extended family. "He doesn't like electricity," she
told them. "He is a man of old-fashioned ways, even if he is an
American." Her family pointed out that Americans weren't supposed to be that way. "Mine is," Maria told them, thus clinching
the argument since no one else in the family had one.

Harry cleaned out the coffeepot, filled it, and put it on the
stove. He opened two bottles of Damm beer to hold them while
the coffee was brewing. Then he looked in the refrigerator for
*tapas*, those delicious little appetizers that the Spanish are always
nibbling at and which may account for the girth of some of the
more prosperous among them.

"Relax," Hob said. "We'll go out for dinner later. Is Juanito's
open?"

"Next week. But La Estrella is open, and there's a new place,
Los Asparagatos, with Italian food. I hear it's pretty good."

"I'll try it out," Hob said. "How's Maria?"

"She's doing just great," Harry said. He and Maria had married just six months previously, in the white-domed San Carlos
church. Hob had been Harry's best man. Maria had looked lovely
in her grandmother's handmade white satin and lace gown. Hob
remembered her face, an olive oval, so much in contrast to Harry's
square, red, American face. Father Gomez, Maria's priest, had of-
ficiated, first making sure that Harry's seldom-practiced Catholi-
cism had not totally lapsed. Harry had promised to do better by
the church in the future. Father Gomez had known he wouldn't,

but protocol had been satisfied, and Gomez, a Catalan from Barcelona, was not one to put up barriers to the achievement of a little happiness on Earth.

"Why didn't you let me know you were coming?" Harry asked.

"No time," Hob said. "I didn't know myself until about five hours ago when I caught a flight out of Paris."

"So what's up?" Harry asked, shaking a cigarette out of his blue-and-white pack of Rumbos extra *largos*.

"There are a couple things I've got to check up on," Hob said.

"Like what?"

"I need to get a line on a man named Stanley Bower."

"I've heard that name. Britisher? Lives on the island, doesn't he?"

"That's right. He was murdered in Paris just three days ago."

Harry nodded. "What's that to us? Was he a client?"

"His brother hired me to find his killer. Also, Fauchon wants me to look into it. He mentioned our license to operate in Paris."

"Gotcha," Harry said. "What do you need to find out about this guy?"

"It'd be nice to learn if he was doing anything here that might have got him killed in Paris. A man named Etienne Vargas, lives on the island, had an appointment to see him. Also there's this: Minutes before Stanley was killed, he was having a drink with a man. Not Vargas. The man walked away. Stanley got it moments later."

"What do you know about this guy he was having the drink with?"

"Very little. Middle-aged guy, brown or tanned face. Wore a ring with a big stone that looked like an emerald. They were speaking in Spanish and English, consulting a Spanish road map that might have been of Ibiza. And our informant thinks the man's name had a rolled Spanish *r* in it."

"That's great," Harry said. "Oughta be able to find him with no difficulty. All right, I'll get on it. There are what? Only about a million Spanish speakers on Ibiza this summer."

"I know it's not much. But we can try. And there's another matter. I need to talk to Kate about some glass bottles."

Harry looked at Hob suspiciously. "You are referring to your ex-wife, Kate?"

Hob nodded.

"Hob, you told me you were through with the lady."

"I am, of course. But there's something I need to find out from her."

"What's that?"

"It concerns Stanley's murder. Ever hear of a drug called soma?"

Harry thought for a while then shook his head.

"Something new," Hob said. "International implications. It could be very big."

"How does that tie in with Stanley Bower?"

"Look, I'll explain everything to you tonight over dinner. Where's Maria?"

"Over in Mallorca. Some celebration of her relatives. Hob, explain it to me now. What is this all about?"

"A little green bottle was found on Stanley's body."

"So what? What's it got to do with you?"

"The French police are very interested in that bottle. There may be others like it. They're wondering who they belonged to, who Stanley got them from."

"Sure. But I still don't see—"

"Harry, the bottle was filled with this soma stuff. And I'm pretty sure it's *my* glass bottle."

Harry Hamm squinted at him. "What in hell are you talking about? Are you sure this was yours?"

"I think so. I had a lot of them, and they were quite distinctive. I picked up a couple gross of them with a shipment of saris from India back when I was a supplier to hippie merchants."

"What did you use them for?"

"Perfume. Cheap essence of jasmine from Kashmir. A good-selling item. But they were also a perfect size for hash oil in gram amounts."

"For Christ's sake, Hob . . ."

"Don't go getting funny with me, Harry. That was a long time ago. I've been legitimate for twenty years. I'd forgotten all about those bottles. But there was a time when they were my trademark. I need to find out who's been using them. Before it gets pinned on me."

"Where did you see them last?"

"I had them stashed away in a shed in my finca."

"What finca was that, Hob?"

"Ca'n Doro, the one Kate's got now."

"I guess you better discuss it with the lady," Harry said.

# 2

KATE'S FINCA WAS in Santa Gertrudis. Hob left Harry's finca and drove out of the mountains to the main road, then through the Morna valley to the main road. He went through Santa Eulalia and picked up the highway to Ibiza. Halfway there, he took a right-hand fork that led to San Antonio Abad. A mile down he turned off to a small finca set back off the road.

There were two cars in the yard, one of them Kate's old blue Citröen, the other a fairly new American Ford station wagon. Hob parked. Already he was feeling all funny in the stomach. That was how he got around Kate.

She was running out of the house and into the yard before he got the car door closed.

"Hob! How wonderful!"

She still looked good. To be accurate, she looked better than ever, wearing a colorful sundress low off the shoulders, her blond hair, dark and gold and gleaming white at the ends, fluffed out and floating in the breeze.

Hob took a deep breath. Easy, boy, he told himself. She always did have your number.

"Hi, Kate. I was passing by, thought I'd drop in, see how you were."

She was a woman of medium height, in her early forties, a sweet face, a smile like a sunburst. Putting on a little weight now but still looking better than good. She exuded that strange odor that memories have, the dark musky kind that are as impossible as they are irresistible. A girl who could model sunshine—that's what he'd called her once upon a time.

"Well, come on in!"

She lead him into the house, a small, modern bungalow. A man stepped out onto the little porch: tall, thin, muscular, small mustache, neat little feet in black moccasins, stylish white clothes, annoyed look on a spoiled brown face.

"Hob, this is Antonio Moreno. I don't know if you know each other. Señor Vargas is a painter who has come here from Madrid. He's quite well known. I know you don't follow art much, but perhaps you heard of his mural of the dead horses in the Gallery Montjuich? They created quite a stir. Señor Vargas has agreed to show me some of his work. I'm working as an agent now for Madras Gallery in La Peña. We're hoping Señor Vargas will let us have some of his paintings on consignment. Señor Vargas, this is Hob Draconian, my ex-husband."

"Harya," Hob snarled.

"*Encantado*," Vargas sneered.

Kate explained to Vargas, "I really need a chance to talk to Hob, Señor Vargas. Could you go back to the hotel for those canvasses you promised to show me and return in half an hour or so?"

"Yes, of course," Moreno said sourly. He left in the American Ford.

Kate led Hob to the comfortable back veranda and poured iced tea for them both. "The children are off in Switzerland with Derek. They'll be disappointed to hear you were here and they didn't see you. Hob, you're looking tired."

"Lack of success is fatiguing," Hob told her. He didn't ask about Derek. Manfully, he resisted asking her whether there was anything between her and Vargas beyond dead horses. She wouldn't tell him, anyway.

"The agency isn't going well?"

"It's going fine, just not making much money."

"Maybe things will pick up," Kate said.

Hob nodded, looking away. The sight of Moreno had soured his day, maybe his month. He didn't like to see any man around

Kate, not even Derek, whom she had lived with for almost five years. He knew he was a fool to think anything might ever be possible again between him and Kate. It was time to take care of his business and get back to Paris. And Marielle. Ugh. To quote Rilke, "You must change your life."

"Look, Kate, I need to ask you about something. Remember those little green glass bottles I used to have? The ones I imported from India back about twenty years ago?"

"Of course I remember," Kate said. "You used them for the hash oil you were selling."

Hob winced. "When you and I split up, I left a lot of those empty bottles, along with some other stuff, out in the back shed."

"You left a lot of junk," Kate said. "You had piles of cowhides out there, and ugly little embroidered purses from India. And feathers; you had bales of feathers."

"Nothing strange about that. I was selling that stuff to hippie merchants, for the weekly bazaar."

"You had all sorts of things. And glass beads—my God but you had glass beads. Let me see, what else was there?"

Kate struck a pose of thinking. She was the most beautiful woman Hob had ever known, and the most exasperating. It was always like this when he needed a simple straight answer to a question, she was off in never-never land with her memories.

"Remember Phillipe?" she asked. "You gave him all your hash pipes."

"Yes, I remember him. He was going to write something about different styles in smoking paraphernelia. But Kate, about the glass bottles . . ."

"I'm thinking," Kate said. She looked at him squarely. "I'm thinking how good we were together back in the old days, Hob."

Hob felt his heart give a sort of convulsive leap of joy, then settle back to its old business of keeping his humdrum life going. They had been good once for about two weeks, bad for about two years; that was the story of Hob and Kate in a nutshell filled with bile.

"Yes, we were good, weren't we?" Hob said. "Too bad Pieter Sommers came along."

"Pieter? You're blaming our breakup on Pieter?"

"I did find you in bed with him."

"Yes, but that was after I found out about your little affair with Soraya."

"Well, what difference did it make? That was the year we were trying our open marriage, remember?"

"The open marriage was only theoretical. We never definitely agreed on it."

Even in a T-shirt, Hob felt hot under the collar. There were memories here he'd forgotten. He didn't want to stir them up. The breakup had been her fault—and if it hadn't, he didn't want to know.

"Theoretical?" Kate said, with a short barking laugh he suddenly remembered all too well. "I suppose Annabelle was theoretical as well?"

"Annabelle? But, Kate, I never had anything with her!"

"That's not what you told me at the time!"

"I was trying to make you jealous."

"Well, you didn't succeed. And anyhow, you'll get your chance all over again. She's living on the island again."

"I don't care where she's living! I never had anything to do with her nor wanted to."

"You always could lie," Kate said. "You and she will have a chance to go over old times now, won't you?"

"What are you talking about? I have no intention of seeing Annabelle!"

"You'd better. She's the one I gave the bottles to."

Hob turned to go, then stopped. "Do you know a man named Etienne Vargas?"

"I've met him once or twice at the beach. Nice boy."

"Do you happen to know where he's staying? I hear his father has a finca on the island."

"So I've heard. But I don't think Etienne is staying there. He's staying with Peter Two, I think."

# 3

PETER TWO WAS Ibiza's second best-known dealer. Peter was a specialist in hashish and a fanatic about quality. He was said to have his own farm in Morocco, where he personally supervised the conversion of marijuana leaf into hashish.

The fact that there was a Peter Two implied that there was a Peter One. The island was divided on the question of who Peter One might be, of if there were anybody of that name. It was believed that Peter Two had taken his name expecting that the police, when they got around to investigating the hashish situation on Ibiza, would look for Number One and leave Two alone. So far it had worked out. Peter Two was doing well and living handsomely.

Not every finca on Ibiza was traditional. Peter Two's farm had been remodeled to give it overhanging roofs that curved up at the ends like a Japanese house out of Kurosawa. The oriental look was further accentuated by the long Tibetan flags set on high bamboo poles that fluttered bravely in the wind that usually blew across the hilltop near San Jose where Peter lived. Inside Peter's house the Japanese motif was further accentuated by the polished hardwood floors, the sparseness of furnishing, the complete lack of clutter, and the bamboo separators that divided room from room and could be taken down to provide larger spaces. Peter Two could afford this affectation of simplicity. The Zen sand garden Hob passed on the way from the driveway to the main building was even more artfully simple: three perfectly placed stones in twenty square yards of raked sand. Hob liked the sight of it very much. Though he couldn't afford to build one himself. Nor did he have the time or manpower to rake the sand every day and take from it every leaf and twig that had blown into it overnight. Hob's own finca was a clutter of objects, and so he always appreciated the luxurious simplicity of Peter's place.

When Hob came to call that morning, no one seemed to be about. Hob hallooed the house, as was customary when making an unexpected call, and, receiving no answer, but noticing that both Peter's and Devi's cars were parked in the front, he came on through to the back. There he found Devi, her masses of dark hair pinned up, wearing a mauve sari, stirring up a batch of zucchini bread for lunch.

"Hi, Hob."

"I called but no one answered."

"I can't hear a thing when I'm in back here. I've told Peter he should put in an intercom system, but Mr. Back To Nature won't hear of it."

"Is the master about?"

"The lord is in the drying shed, communing with his spirits."

"I wouldn't want to bother him."

"Go right on back. It's time Peter and his spirits had someone new to talk to."

Devi was small and lovely, with black hair that showed hennaed red highlights. She was an exotic even on an island of exotics, daughter of a British dam builder on contract to the government of Rajaspur and a light-skinned princess of the Rajputs, or so she claimed. It was difficult to know the truth about anyone's background on Ibiza, since people made up stories that suited their fantasies about themselves.

Hob followed the stone steps that led through the bamboo grove and around the small frog pond to the drying shed in the rear of the property. Here was where the Ibicencos had stored their *algorobos*, and where Peter stored his marijuana, his incomparable homegrown stuff. Peter Two was a dope dealer by occupation and a connoisseur of dope as a hobby.

He looked up now when Hob came in. He had been pruning

one of his large potted marijuana plants with embroidery scissors, and he had a nice little pile of golden-green leaves on a clean silk cloth. There was another man with him, a very tall young man with a dark café au lait skin whom Hob had met sometime before at a party. He was from Brazil and was reputed to be wealthy, or at least to have a wealthy father, and had been going with Annabelle, who lived somewhere in Ibiza City.

Hob had come by to ask if Peter was planning to start the class in Buddhist meditation that he had been sponsoring. In Ibiza, a place without telephones except in commercial businesses at that time, if you wanted to find something out, you drove to where you could ask the question in person, unless you wanted to wait until you ran across the person at some coffee shop or restaurant or on one of the beaches. This could take quite a long time, however, so if you really wanted an answer within a week or so, you drove to where the person lived.

"I'm going to have to delay again," Peter said. "Sunny Jim agreed to teach the course, but he's off in Barcelona getting motorcycle parts for his shop."

"Okay," Hob said. "I'd appreciate if you'd get word to me when it does begin."

"Count on it," Peter said.

"I wanted to ask you," Hob said. "Have you ever heard of a drug called soma?"

"Of course I've heard of it," Peter said. "It was a classical drug of ancient India. Also a god. Why?"

"There's some talk it's being made currently."

"I doubt that very much," Peter said. "There's never been a formula for it. No one's got any idea what went into it. Someone's pulling your leg, my friend."

"That's not what the Paris police think," Hob said.

"The French are a hysterical race," Peter said sententiously. "France is the original home of the conspiracy theory. It all began with the Knights Templar. Etienne, you ever hear of this stuff?"

"Never have," Etienne said. "But if it's going around I'd like some. What was that about the French police, Hob?"

"Well, it's no secret that Stanley Bower was killed in Paris this week. The French believe he was selling some drug called soma."

"I hope they're wrong," Peter said.

"Why?" Hob asked.

"Something new and flashy like that could play hell with my business."

Etienne said, "I'm going to see if Devi will make me a glass of tea. Catch you guys later."

He left, ambling up the sunlit courtyard. Peter busied himself rolling a joint from the marijuana he had just clipped. He did it in the West Indian style, using five papers and coming up with something that looked like a cigar. Neither he nor Hob talked while he was rolling, for rolling a joint was almost a religious rite with Peter, who was one of the best-known dope dealers on the island but didn't like to talk about it.

The joint completed, Peter gave it to Hob to begin. Hob lit the end carefully with a wooden match, took four or five tokes, coughed appreciatively and passed the joint to Peter. Peter toked. They both settled down in the big wicker chairs Peter had provided in the drying shed. For a while they didn't talk. The first smoke of the day was a sacred moment.

Finally, Peter said, "How's the agency going?"

"Pretty well," Hob said.

After that they smoked, and there was no need for further conversation. Half an hour later Hob was on his way back to his finca, pleasantly stoned, with one of Peter's one-ounce Temple Balls, made of the finest Pakistani hashish and wrapped in the bright blue cellophane that was Peter's trademark. It was a present worth having. Peter had done so well in the dope trade in the last year that he hardly bothered selling his Temple Balls, reserving them as gifts for special friends.

# 4

INVESTIGATING SOMEONE IN Ibiza can be as simple or as complicated as you care to make it. If the investigatee lived in the village of Santa Eulalia, the first thing to do was to go to El Kiosko, the big open-air café in the center of town. El Kiosko occupied the upper portion of a large rectangle of tiled ground that led down to the sea. The café was on the upper portion, near the statue of Abel Matutes.

It didn't take Hob long to get a line on Stanley Bower. The guy was a member of the permanent British house guest set, always broke—"just a little stony, old boy"—but always wearing good clothes, which were to the professional house guest as hex wrenches were to the auto mechanic. Good shoes were important, too. Stanley Bower would always be remembered for his collection of Bally's. And he had a gold Audemars Piguet watch—probably a Hong Kong copy, but you can't go opening up the back of a man's watch to prove it.

Hob was making his investigation at a good time. It was late afternoon, just before the stores opened again after the siesta. A cross-section of expatriates from the area were at the café, with their straw baskets crouched at their feet like hungry dogs, waiting to be filled with the evenings' provisions.

Tomas the Dane was at a center table, tall and blond with his usual small dark blue captain's hat. "Stanley? Sure, I saw him last week. Went off to Paris, so I hear. He owe you money?"

"Not exactly. I need his assistance in my investigations." That

brought a big laugh from Tomas and his friends. At that time nobody took Hob's detective agency seriously. That was to come
later, after the old Italian guy with the price on his head came to
the island.

"You might want to check with his old lady," Tomas said.

"Who's that?" Hob asked.

"Annabelle. The one from London, not the French Annabelle.
You know her, don't you, Hob?"

"Sure I do. But I didn't know she was Stanley's old lady. How
is she?"

"Still shooting up, so I hear," Tomas said. "Still pretty as a picture and twisted as a braid."

"Where's she living these days?"

"Damned if I know. Not in Santa Eulalia. But Big Bertha would
know. You know where Big Bertha lives?"

"I imagine she's still in the D'Alt Villa," Hob said. "Listen,
Tomas, Harry ought to be down here later for a beer. Tell him I'll
have to take a rain check on our dinner tonight. Tell him I'll try
to see him sometime tonight at Sandy's."

Hob drove his rented car to Ibiza City, but parked on the out-
skirts near the motorcycle shop and walked into town to the cab
rank on the Alameda. It just wasn't worth trying to drive that last
part, there was no parking up in the D'Alt Villa anyhow. The big
black-and-white Mercedes taxi took him down La Calle de las Far-
macias, then made the right turn that led through the Roman
wall to the D'Alt Villa. This was the highest part of the city, and
the oldest. The road wound up narrow, precipitous streets without sidewalks, up past the museum, then made another turn into
the highest part of the city. Here the taxi stopped. Hob paid and
got out and proceeded on foot through passageways scarcely
wide enough for two men to pass abreast.

Big Bertha lived on a nameless alley in the D'Alt Villa, just a
stone's throw below the highest point of the Old City. Ibiza was
filled with foreigners snobbish about where they lived, and certain that their location was superior to all others. The smaller the
island, the more choosy the foreigners were about where they
lived on it. In Ibiza every part of the island had its adherents, with

the possible exception of the garbage dump, a noiseome smouldering Dantean sort of place on the old road through Jesus.

The D'Alt Villa had its old gracious apartments situated in fine old buildings. There were a few trees up there, and good air. The only difficulty was getting there. The climb was steep, there were no buses, and not even taxis could negotiate the final part. Big Bertha solved the problem by never leaving her apartment except to go to a nearby restaurant or to a new showing at the Sims Gallery just down the street, or to any party anywhere on the island. Even that much was an effort. Big Bertha weighed just under three hundred pounds. She was a jolly American woman, some said related to the Du Ponts of Delaware. She had lived in Ibiza forever, under the republic, the Franco government, and the republic again. She had known Elliot Paul. She was social, loved people, adored music. And she was wealthy. The income from the Du Ponts, or, more likely, some less famous but equally solvent industrial family, allowed her to live in style and entertain with distinction. She gave a party almost every month, befriended artists of all sorts and every degree of talent and pretension, made small loans to some, let others use the small finca she owned out on the island in the parish of San Juan. It was said that she knew everybody on the island. That was not possible. During a tourist season, a million people might pass in and out of Son San Juan airport. But she knew a lot of people, and the ones she didn't know she could find out about if she cared to.

She greeted Hob in her flowering muumuu and led him into the apartment. It was large and airy, filled with a complication of couches, cane-backed chairs, Ibicenco chests, breakfronts, tables, and a couple of large cracked-and-mended pointed-bottomed Roman amphorae in iron stands. She led him to her breezy terrace. The light was golden on the dark earth-red tiles. Below, the city of Ibiza fell away in a series of swaybacked cubistic white squares and rectangles, all the way to the harbor with its several cruise ships and countless cafés.

"So," she said after a few minutes of desultory chat, "what brings you to my aerie?"

"I'm looking for Annabelle," Hob said. "I was hoping you could tell me where she lives these days."

"I could probably find out," Bertha said. "Give me a couple of days, I'll ask some people. What else is happening with you? Are you here on a case, or just hanging out like the rest of us?"

"I'm looking into Stanley Bower's murder. You heard of that?"

Bertha nodded. "Laurent telephoned from Paris. He read about it in the *Herald Trib*. He was utterly prostrated."

"I heard that Annabelle was seeing a lot of Stanley."

"She went to some parties with him, but you know Stanley wasn't interested in girls."

"So I heard. But they were friends anyway."

"No crime in that, is there?"

Hob decided to try a different tack. "Bertha, how'd you like to work for me?"

"Me, work as a private investigator?"

"An assistant to a private investigator. Yes, that's exactly what I mean."

Big Bertha smiled and shook her head in amazement but she didn't say no. She got up, went to the sideboard and fixed two gin and sodas. Hob knew she didn't need the money. She was doing all right with her bar, her restaurant. She even had a few investments, owned some property. But Bertha was a busybody, she was nosy, she liked to find out things, she loved to gossip. This could give her a reason that made it okay for her to gossip.

She returned with the drinks, handed one to Hob. "What'll I have to do?"

"Just what you're doing now. Seeing people. Giving parties. Going to art gallery openings. Eating in good restaurants. I can't pay for that, of course. But it's what you do anyhow. And then you talk to me."

"Sure. No problem there."

Hob had learned that people, even great gossips, were more motivated when they're being paid to talk, even if that pay was only a pittance. The act of payment seemed to put a stamp of approval on what otherwise might have seemed a light-minded activity. And to give it a stamp of usefulness, of social use, of propriety. And even the most outrageous were not about to turn away from a little propriety when it came attached to some money.

"Sounds like fun." Even Big Bertha liked the idea of being a useful citizen if it could be made amusing and if it paid. But it didn't have to pay much. And that was good because Hob didn't have much. Everyone knew his agency was more an idée fixe than a going proposition. But what could be more attractive than an idée fixe, even if you weren't a French decadent, as long as it didn't involve too much work and paid enough to make it respectable?

"What do you want me to do, Hob? I'm not so mobile these days, you know."

"The great thing about this, Bertha, is that you don't have to change what you're doing one bit."

"What do you want, specifically?"

"There's a man I need to get a line on. Learn who he is and whatever you can find out about him." Hob told her the story of the man who was last seen with Stanley Bower in Paris and gave what he had of a description.

"Not much to go on," Bertha said.

"If anyone can put a name and identity to this man, it's you."

"You flatter me, Hob. But you're right. If I or some of the people I know don't know this guy, he doesn't exist."

She thought a moment, then said, "You want information? I love to give information. Why should you pay me for it?"

"Useful services deserve to be paid for," Hob said. "And I like to employ my friends. That's the ideal of the Alternative Detective Agency."

"It's a noble ideal."

"I think so."

"And a little foolish, as noble ideals so often are."

Hob shrugged. "Do you want the job or not?"

"Hell, yes," Bertha said. "I'd be delighted to work as one of your operatives. What else do you want to know right now?"

Hob looked baffled. He wasn't used to this much directness. He had to think for a minute. After a moment or two he said, "Well, aside from Annabelle's whereabouts and the identity of the mysterious Spanish speaker, what's new in Ibiza? I mean, is there anything new?"

"There's always new stuff going on here," Bertha said. "You mean like gallery openings or new boutiques?"

"I don't think so," Hob said. "Something else."

"You aren't very specific. . . . What about the new hotel?"

"Is there a new hotel?"

"I'm amazed you haven't heard about it."

"I've been in Paris."

"That must account for it. Well, there's this new luxury hotel near San Mateo. It's going to open soon. In about two weeks, as a matter of fact. Japanese backers, so I hear. There's going to be a big reception next Wednesday."

"Are you going?"

"Of course. I'm on the B list."

"Is there more than one guest list?"

"My dear, of course! Don't you know how these things work? There's a general reception first for a lot of people. That'll be in the late afternoon on the hotel grounds. Half the island will be there. Anyone can get in, even without an invitation. That's the C list. Then, in the evening, after the hoi polloi have cleared out, there's an exclusive reception, dinner, and dancing for about a hundred or so people."

"And that's the A list?"

"No, my dear, that's the B list. But it's still very grand."

"So what's the A list?"

"After the B list people have cleared out, probably sometime after midnight, about eight or ten people remain. They're the owners and investors, and their ladies, of course—or their lads, as the case may be. Then there's drinking and drugging until dawn. The A list isn't as much fun as the B list, except for the snob appeal. If you're not an investor or a boyfriend or girlfriend of an investor, there's no way to get into that one."

"Who are the investors?" Hob asked. "Who's putting up this place?"

"I only know the rumors. The investors are supposed to be a few wealthy Japanese and a few rich South Americans. Rumor hath it that the main financing is coming from the Yakuza—the Japanese criminal element, you know—but of course you'd know that—as one of their overseas investments. Interested?"

"Quite interested," Hob said. "Can you get me and Harry Hamm onto the B list?"

"I can arrange it," Bertha said. "I work for you now; my contacts are your contacts. By the way, not that it's important, but how much do I get?"

"I can't know that until I see how many operatives work on it. You'll get a percentage of the take based on how much time you put in on the case and how much bodily danger you run, if any."

"Well, whatever," Bertha said. "No bodily danger, though, if you don't mind. I'll get on to that South American who knew Stanley. By the way, you'll find Annabelle in the Beehive in Figueretas."

"I thought you said you'd have to check around and see."

"That was before you hired me, dear heart. I was going to check first to see if she wanted to see you. Now it doesn't matter."

# 5

Hob walked downhill to Ibiza and out of the city to his car. He got in and drove past the dreary new construction and around to the far side of the city, where Figueretas lay.

He followed the unpaved road out of the city and went down a long bumpy road with the sea on one side and pastel-colored hotels lining the other side. This was the new Ibiza. Unlike the Dalt Villa, no ancient Roman wall surrounded Figueretas. It stood by itself just before Salinas, the ancient Roman salt flats, still being worked.

Figueretas had been overlooked in the general wave of prosperity that had come to Ibiza. It was a neighborhood of rundown little bars and tiny food stores and seedy restaurants, catering to a variegated crowd of middle-class losers, dopers, drinkers, and remittance men, burned-out musicians, decrepit card sharks, absconding businessmen, and the like.

The Beehive was three rickety four-story structures with outside staircases, the buildings laced together with walkways and laundry lines. The view of the sea on the other side of the breakwater was splendid but distant.

Annabelle lived on the *tercero piso* of building *dos*. Hob went up the steps past back doors crowded with garbage and old baby carriages. Children were screaming at cats, guys were shouting at their old ladies, old ladies were screeching at phantoms of the past, and drunken poets were putting it all down in incomprehensible verses high on strained imagery. It was one of those European-style *Porgy and Bess* scenes.

Annabelle said, "Come in and take a load off your feet, Hob. Want a beer?"

"Sure," Hob said.

The apartment was small and unkempt. The best thing about it was its view of low buildings along Ibiza's shoreline and the deep turquoise of the sea itself. The large casement window was open. A light breeze came through, fluttering the laundry that Annabelle had strung out on a line on the open veranda. The apartment itself smelled of cat. Annabelle's old tortoiseshell cat, Santana, sat on the back of one of the sagging overstuffed chairs and glared at Hob. Smell of cat mingled with the smells of olive oil and garlic and laundry soap. Annabelle herself was wearing a silk kimono, or maybe it was nylon—Hob wasn't up on these distinctions. Whatever it was, it was brightly colored in reds and oranges. The front sagged open revealing plenty of Annabelle's full, pointed, slightly sagging breasts. When she crossed her legs the kimono fell away revealing a long streak of tan thigh. She was far and away the best looking junkie on the island, a Londoner from somewhere near Swiss Cottage, in her late twenties, with features that vaguely reminded Hob of a young Joan Collins. She'd first come to Ibiza in her teens and taken up with Black Roger, a heroin dealer from Detroit. They'd had some good times together until Roger got busted in the first big police cleanup of dealers, out-of-control junkies, and other undesirables. Annabelle had always been able to take junk or leave it. But that ability was beginning to leave her. Her arms were still free of tracks—she was vain about her small, well-shaped body and injected between her toes.

"What're you up to these days?" Hob asked.

Annabelle shrugged. "Waitressing at Dirty Domingo's. It's a bitch of a job, but it'll do until I can sell some paintings."

Among other things, Annabelle was a painter. Her childish daubs, which she called primitives, of old Ibicenco ladies working in the fields with sheep in the background, painted without perspective, had enjoyed a brief vogue in the island's art galleries until even more primitive painters crowded her out with even more striking lack of perspective. There was always a lot of competition among primitive artists on Ibiza.

"What about you?" Annabelle said. She rose and went to the refrigerator, opened it, and took out two bottles of San Miguel beer. Hob regretted accepting when the refrigerator let out a fetid odor of last week's lamb-and-garbanzo stew. "You still doing the detective agency?"

Hob nodded. Businesses among the expatriates of Ibiza were so rare that everyone stayed informed on how it was going for the enterprising few, the better to get a loan during their brief periods of prosperity.

"Are you working on something now?"

Hob nodded. "I am helping the French police in their investigations."

"So this is a business trip?"

"It has to do with Stanley Bower. Can you tell me anything about Stanley's recent business dealings?"

"Oh, Hob, you are a bit of a dope. Lovable, but silly. Why on earth should I tell you anything about Stanley, if I knew anything, which I don't?"

"Is there any reason you shouldn't tell me?"

"I suppose not. But I don't want to get into any trouble."

"Annabelle, I'm an old friend. Tell me everything. I won't pass anything on. I'll protect you."

"I know you will, Hob. As well as you're able. But why don't you ask Stanley?"

"I can't. He's dead, Annabelle."

She looked at him wide-eyed. "Dead? Really?"

Hob nodded.

"How?"

Hob told her how Bower was killed in Paris.

Annabelle thought for a while, then shook her head. "Hob, I'd be glad to tell you whatever I remember. But not here. Take me to dinner at El Olivo's, and I'll sing like a canary. Wait just a moment while I change."

*    *    *

"Have you ever tried their caviar blinis?" Annabelle said, an hour later, as they sat on the terrace of El Olivo, on one of the intermediate levels of the steep Old City. "It's real caviar, Hob, not that dreadful Danish lumpfish." Hob noted that she had made a quick recovery from the news of Stanley's death.

"Real caviar? Oh, good," Hob said. "I was a little worried about that."

They both greeted the eight or ten friends who strolled by on the errands that take up so much of the Ibiza day and night. After a couple of shots of the house vodka, Annabelle was ready to talk.

"I was spending some time with Stanley Bower up until last month," she said. "We went to a few parties together. This was after I broke up with Etienne. We didn't do anything—he was gay, you know. And now he's dead. I don't like to talk about him much."

Hob waited. Annabelle smiled and ordered a champagne cocktail from a hovering waiter.

"That's all?" Hob asked. "I could have found that out from anyone for the price of a cognac."

"Well, that's not my fault, is it? Go on, ask something else."

"When did you see Stanley last?"

Annabelle thought for a moment, biting one long red fingernail. "I guess it was the night before he left for Paris. We had dinner together at Arlene's."

"Did he mention why he was going to Paris?"

"He said he had to take care of something there, but he didn't say what."

"And then?"

"I suppose he was going to come back here. But I don't know."

"Did he seem worried, anxious?"

"Stanley? He didn't look like he had a care in the world."

"Just great," Hob said. "Do you remember seeing him with a tanned or dark-skinned man, probably a Spanish speaker, probably Spanish or South American, with a big emerald ring and a name with a rolled Spanish *r* in it?"

"No, nobody like that."

"You answered too quickly," Hob said.

"What do you mean?"

"I mean you didn't think about it first. That leads me to think you know who I mean."

"I don't. I know Stanley's crowd. Mainly French and English. Not a Latino in the bunch."

"Maybe you should have another champagne cocktail."

"I will, never fear. Waiter!"

"Did you know what Bower was going to do in Paris?"

"Hob, I didn't know the guy at all well. We just laughed a lot together. Why are you asking me all these questions?"

Hob lit a Rumbo, coughed, and took a sip of his San Miguel beer. "I wish you hadn't asked that. I was hoping to trap you into a damaging admission."

"Well, out with it, what's this all about?"

"The French police are interested."

"Are they? Is there a reward?"

"Annabelle, if there were a reward, I'd have told you straight out. If there is one, I'll see you get it. But you better talk to me about Stanley. You like to go to Paris from time to time, don't you?"

"Sure. What are you talking about?"

"The guy investigating this case, Inspector Fauchon, will see to it personally that you get a lot of plain French hellishness if you don't cooperate. You'll get picked up and questioned when you come to Paris. He could even make you some trouble here."

Annabelle considered it calmly. "I could just never go to Paris."

"So you could. But why should you want never to come to Paris if you've got nothing to hide?"

Annabelle hesitated, thought it over. "Hob, I'm really not clever enough to lie to you. I don't know a thing. Christ! Stanley dead! What lousy luck!"

"I don't know if it was a matter of luck," Hob said.

"I mean my luck, not his. Stanley never had any luck. I should have known better than to loan him three hundred pounds for this stupid trip of his."

"Get your wrap, Annabelle," Hob said. "Time we were going."

The bill came to a hundred and seventy-three dollars, not including the tip that Hob forgot to leave. The champagne, of course, was extra.

# 6

THERE WAS A cab stand outside the restaurant, in the little plaza with the hippie shoemaker shop on the corner. Hob put Annabelle into a taxi and gave her a thousand peseta note for the fare. He'd had enough of her for the night. Then he walked through the narrow alley that led to the parking lot at the back of the restaurant where he'd left his rental car. The parking lot was an irregular rectangle outlined by whitewashed stones. When Hob entered it he saw there was someone sitting on the fender of his SEAT, smoking a cigarette. The cigarette glowed red in the darkness as the man puffed on it then flipped it away.

"Hey," the man said, "you're Hob Draconian, aren't you?"

"Who are you?" Hob asked.

"I wouldn't worry too much about that," the man said, getting to his feet. He started walking toward Hob. There was something about the way he moved that Hob didn't like. Hob started backing away slowly, wishing that he was the sort of detective who carried a gun. That was not so easy in Europe, but at least he could have had a knife or blackjack. As it was he had nothing but a ballpoint pen. And even that was in an inside pocket where he couldn't get at it easily. The man was still coming toward him in what could be described as a threatening manner. Hob looked around. There was nobody in sight, and even if there had been, he wouldn't have seen them for it was pitch black. The heavy bass of the rock music coming from El Olivo was sure to drown out any hysterical screams for help he might make.

He took two steps backward, prepared to wheel and run back to the restaurant for his life. And then he heard a sound on the left side of him. He turned. There was a man walking out from between two cars, buttoning up his fly.

"Listen," Hob said to the newcomer, "We have some trouble here."

"Yes, I am part of it," the newcomer said.

Hob wasn't slow. He saw at once that the two men were working together.

"What do you guys want?" Hob asked, hoping his voice wasn't quavering.

The first man, larger of the two, was dressed in dark clothing and had on a stupid little Tyrolean hat with a silver-mounted fox brush in its sweatband. He said, "We been told you been sticking your nose into matters that are none of your concern. We're here to talk to you about that." He had an accent, probably South American.

His companion, small and venemous, with tiny ferret teeth gleaming above a dark shirt and white necktie and steel-capped shoes, said, "We goin' to make our point in the heavily physical style we understand best." Another Latino, probably uneducated, but with an ornate delivery.

While they talked both men were herding Hob along in a businesslike way. They had him in a narrow alley between cars, behind which was a ten-foot-high stone wall, and beyond that a straight drop down the side of the city. There was nowhere for Hob to go but straight ahead, into their arms. That didn't seem a likely route. He was definitely in trouble.

Then Hob heard the sound of a car door opening. They all turned and watched as a man stepped out of a big, dusty old Mercedes. All Hob could make out at first was dark trousers and a dark shirt. As the man approached, Hob could see that he had curly white hair, the only light thing in the surroundings. He walked toward them, saying, "Mr. Draconian?"

"I'd love to talk to you some other time," Hob said. "For now, why don't you run like mad out of here and call the cops, and maybe have them send an ambulance, too."

"Yeah, buddy," the larger South American said. "Why don't you get your ass the hell out of here?"

"I have need to talk to Mr. Draconian," the stranger said. "My business is pressing."

The smaller man laughed—a short ugly sound from a short ugly man. "Pressing? Listen, baby, you want pressing, we'll give you pressing." He started to walk toward the whitehaired stranger, who was standing in a little space between cars, illuminated now by stray beams from a vagrant three-quarter moon drifting lazily between wispy clouds.

The stranger said, in conversational tones, "Mr. Vargas is arriving tomorrow."

The two men stopped, but only for a moment. The bigger one said, "So what's that to us?"

"He wants everything to stay nice and quiet."

"It'll be nice and quiet by the time he gets here," the bigger man said. "Now, get the hell out of here. We have business with this guy."

"No," the white-haired stranger said. "Forget your business and go away."

The South Americans started to move again, approaching the white-haired stranger from different sides. Hob was getting ready to throw himself into action, as soon as he could control the violent quavering in his knees. The stranger was up on his toes, bouncing lightly, and then he was moving toward the big one, taking quick little dancing steps. The little rat-faced guy was taking something from his pocket—gun, knife, or razor, Hob couldn't tell what it was in the darkness. But no matter, because the stranger suddenly turned, rocked back on one leg and kicked, a beautiful kick, like a soccer sweeper. The toe of his shoe caught the object and sent it spinning into the darkness, to land with a metallic clang on the roof of a distant car.

"Wha' the fuck?" the big man said. He put down his bullet head and charged, but the white-haired man was turning, pirouetting in a weird sort of ballet movement, dancing and darting to one side, and his hands flashed out, making sharp, snapping sounds as they came into contact with the big man's shoulder and head. The guy was stopped dead in his tracks. He took a clumsy off-balance swipe at the stranger, but the man was already out of range, dancing on his toes, coming at the smaller man, moving past him and catching him in the *kishkes* with a vicious elbow blow. The little guy bellowed and swung his fists. The stranger pirouetted again, and his foot lashed out behind him. He caught the little guy in the pit of the stomach. The little guy made an obscene sound as all the air was forcibly expelled from his body. He fell backward, making horrible retching sounds as he tried to catch his breath. The stranger tiptoed in again coming toward the other man, his arms whirring in a blur of motion, his legs kicking out. Suddenly the big guy seemed to go airborne. For a moment his body was horizontal to the ground and at right angles to the white-haired stranger, and then he came down hard on the back of his head. He lay there, groaning through bloodied teeth, looking like a gigantic beetle with a South American accent who'd been flipped over onto his back and crushed.

The white-haired stranger turned. The big guy had scrambled back to his feet, but he was not renewing the attack; he was running. The little guy hobbled after him a moment later.

"I think we are finished now," the stranger said.

"Thank you," Hob said, resisting the impulse to throw himself at the stranger's feet and kiss the top of his soft-soled shoes for saving, if not his life, at least his hide and hump. "Might I inquire your name?"

"Of course. I am Juan Braga, but everyone calls me Vana."

Braga! With a rolled Spanish *r*! No emerald ring, but he might have taken it off while showering and forgotten to put it back on. Still, Hob decided not to jump too immediately to conclusions. Lots of Spanish names had an *r* in them. It was one of the popular letters all over the world, except possibly in Japan.

"I haven't seen you around," Hob said.

"That is because I spend most of my time at the finca."

"Which finca is that?"

"Ca'n Soledad. It belongs to Silverio Vargas, my patron."

"Vargas. He got a son named Etienne?"

"Yes, that is correct."

"Small world," Hob said, superfluously, because Ibiza was a very small world, though it seemed to expand a lot once you were living in it.

# 7

HOB ENJOYED A good night's sleep that night, in his own bed in his own bedroom in his own finca, with the branches of the almond tree outside his window making soothing sounds at his window. In the morning he shaved and dressed in clean Lois jeans and a three-button blue Rastro T-shirt and went down to the kitchen to make himself some breakfast. The *butano* was empty, and the spare bottle hadn't been refilled. He put both of the big orange bottles in the back of his car and drove to Anita's for his breakfast. He ate in the outer courtyard, under the shade of the vines that had been trained to crisscross the open rafters of the low roof. After finishing he exchanged the empty *butanos* for full ones at Pablo's general store next door, but decided not to go right back to the finca. He considered driving to Harry Hamm's finca, but decided he'd likely see him in El Kiosko in Santa Eulalia. He drove to the town, found a parking place near Humberto's Hamburguesas, and walked to the Kisoko. Harry was there, just finishing his ham and eggs and reading a three day old *Paris Herald Tribune*. Hob sat down and joined him for a *café con leche*.

"So what's new?" Harry asked.

Hob told him about the previous night with Annabelle and the two guys in the parking lot and his white-haired rescuer. "Said his name was Juan Braga but everyone called him Vana. Ring a bell?"

"Never heard of him," Harry said.

"He told the two guys that Silverio Vargas was arriving on the island today. That was supposed to mean something, though it didn't seem to impress them. Ever hear of him?"

Harry shook his head. "The only news I got is a letter from Maria. She's having a good time in Mallorca and coming back the day after tomorrow. What now?"

Hob tried to look keen, but the calm life of the island was already getting to him. "I think it might be well to await developments. What did Fritz Perls say? Don't push the river."

"That could be the motto of the island," Harry said. "Want to go to Agua Blanca this afternoon?"

"Yes," Hob said. "I can't remember when I was on a beach last. We'll have lunch right there at La Terraza."

"Fine," Harry said. "Let's meet at the Agua Blanca road and just take one car down that goat track."

"We'll take mine," Hob said. "It's only a rental. See you in about two hours. I've got some work to do."

"What work is that?" Harry asked.

"I need to pick up my laundry and buy some club soda and take my *butanos* home. The labor never ends."

Hob finished his chores and was waiting at the Agua Blanca road when Harry drove up. Harry had brought blankets and a few paperbacks. They transferred them to Hob's SEAT and drove down the bumpy dirt track that wound through the lower hills and came out at last at the parking space above Agua Blanca. They took their stuff, stopped at the restaurant to reserve a table and order lunch in an hour, and continued down to the beach. It was a glorious day of blue sky and small white clouds and the blue-green ocean and the tanned bodies of bathers scattered here and there across the two-mile-long beach. They parked under a straw umbrella, for which they paid one of the urchins whose job that was, spread out their towels, and lay until they were hot. Then they went for a swim, then came out to heat up again. This routine, repeated twice, brought them to lunch hour. At La Terraza they had the fish fry, a mixed batch of whatever the fishermen had brought in that day, with rough island bread, olive oil and olives, and a couple of San Miguels to wash it all down. Then they returned to the beach, took a dip, and napped under the umbrella for several hours. It was one of those perfect inconsequential days that were the essence of the Ibizan summer life—for foreigners, that is, since Ibicencos didn't go near the water except to fish in it.

Hob drove Harry back to where he had left his car and arranged to have dinner with him later. He returned to his finca, showered quickly (the gravity-flow tank hadn't been pumped for two days), shaved, and dressed for the evening. He drove back into Santa Eulalia and went to Sandy's. Checking his mail, he found a note from Big Bertha, delivered by one of her friends coming into Santa Eulalia. "Got stuff to talk about. Come see me in the morning." He folded the note and put it into his pocket. Chances were only a few dozen people had read it before he came in. Harry arrived soon after. They had a couple of drinks, then joined several of their friends for dinner, a satisfying lobster mayonnaise at Juanito's. They had a final nightcap at The Black Cat and then home to bed.

# 8

"HOB," BERTHA SAID next morning, over breakfast, after he had come to visit her, "do I get an expense account?"

"What do you need one for?"

"I've already run up some expenses."

"Make a note of it when you hand in your paperwork. Just kidding. What expenses?"

"I bribed somebody. That's the thing an operative's assistant does, isn't it?"

"Depends on what you found out."

"Well, it's going to cost you two thousand pesetas. That's what I laid out in drinks for Dolores."

"Who's Dolores?"

"She's a waitress. Works at Dirty Domingo's. She has a little apartment right next to Annabelle's."

"No problem," Hob said, peeling some thousand peseta bills from his pocket. "What did you learn?"

Bertha tucked the money into her Ibiza basket. She was beaming. "I really feel like an operative now. This is the most exciting thing I've done since my first acid trip."

"I can't tell you how pleased I am at that," Hob said. "Now, if you're finished gloating, would you mind telling me what you've got?"

"Nothing much," Bertha said archly. "Only the identity of that fellow you've been trying to trace. The one who was with Stanley Bower in Paris."

Bertha told Hob what Dolores had told her. She had been out on her front terrace laying out a wash when a man arrived at Annabelle's apartment. This was on the day after Stanley had left for Paris. The stranger was not very tall, but burly, with a tanned dark skin and what Dolores described as "evil eyes," though she did not explain in what respect. Annabelle had not seemed to know the man, but she let him in. By going to her rear terrace with the rest of her laundry, Dolores was able to hear the tone of the conversation, if not the actual words. It had not been amicable. The man had raised his voice. He had been speaking Spanish. Annabelle, replying in English, had seemed to be protesting. Dolores was certain she had heard the sound of a slap, then a cry from Annabelle. Then more conversation, this time lower pitched and urgent. Dolores had been considering leaving her apartment and finding someone who might help—there was a Guardia Civil barracks only half a mile away—when the man came out, slamming the door behind him. He got into a car parked down the block and drove away in the direction of San Antonio, the opposite direction from Ibiza City.

"Did she notice if he had on an emerald ring?" Hob asked.

"She didn't mention it when she told me the story. But when I asked her she said yes, she thought so."

"And what about the name?"

"The only words Dolores was able to make out were Annabelle saying, 'Arranque—please, don't!' It was after that he slapped her."

"Arranque?"

"That's what she heard. Or thought she heard."

"You've done very well," Hob said. "It's a long way from a positive identification, but at least I've something to go on."

"Can I get you a drink?" Bertha asked. "I'm positively aglow with excitement."

"A coffee would be nice."

Hob followed her into the tiled kitchen. While she prepared the pot, he said, "Annabelle, told me she had been going with Etienne. Do you know anything about that?"

"Of course I do," Bertha said. "Milk? Sit down right there and

I'll tell you. Etienne is the French name of a Brazilian boy who is staying on the island. The first thing you should know about Etienne is that he's beautiful."

"And the second thing?"

"That he's rich. Or rather, potentially rich. Give me a cigarette and let me tell you the tale."

When Annabelle and Etienne met at a party at Ursula Oglethorpe's new townhouse near Santa Gertrudis, it was lust at first sight. These two beautiful, uninhibited people were made for each other—at least for that month. And it was springtime in Ibiza, with everyone sick of winter and prepared for summer romance. Etienne had just flown in from Rio de Janeiro. He and Annabelle looked at each other over fluted glasses of champagne, and the game was on.

They did all the fun things together: went to the discos, picnicked on the beaches, drank in the quaint little bodegas of the old city, visited Tanit's cave, looked at the sunset from Vedra, walked along the old Roman wall and saw the cruise ships far below in the harbor like tiny toys on a wrinkled green sea.

When the pleasures of the island began to pall, they availed themselves of Etienne's unlimited airline pass and went on a trip to Biarritz, Santander, Juan-les-Pins, and then across the Atlantic to Jamaica and even Havana. When they came back, something seemed to have changed. An experienced eye like Bertha's could tell that a certain disenchantment had set in. Annabelle never told Bertha exactly what had gone wrong. But within a week, she was seeing Stanley Bower and no longer seeing Etienne. Soon after that, Stanley left for Paris. Etienne had retired to his father's villa in the mountains above San Juan and had not been seen much of late. And that's where the matter stood.

# 9

AFTER SHOWERING AND changing into the easy-fitting white garments customary for a summer evening, Hob left his finca and drove into Santa Eulalia. Finding a parking place only with difficulty, he walked back to Sandy's, through the violet sunset. Inside Sandy's, one platoon of the usual crowd was there. Sandy's record player played baroque melodies of the Renaissance. Ice tinkled in Bloody Marys and gin fizzes. Diffracted light shone through woven straw baskets shielding low-wattage lightbulbs.

Hob pushed his way through the crowd, dense in the small room, and checked the mail piled up on the counter next to the bar. He wasn't expecting anything, but you could never tell. He was surprised to find a flimsy blue envelope postmarked Paris. Opening it, he found a money order in the amount of ten thousand francs and a note. It was from Jean-Claude. The note said, with Jean-Claude's customary succinctness, "Here is a partial payment on latest agency deal. Nigel has filled you in on details by now. He is also taking care of the other matter."

Nigel in Paris? What agency deal? What other matter? Hob's pleasurable reaction to the arrival of unexpected money—one of the greatest pleasures known to modern man—was clouded only by the unpleasant feeling that something important was going on that he didn't know anything about.

He checked through the mail again, hoping to find an explanatory letter. Nothing. He caught Sandy's attention and asked if there had been a telephone call for him recently.

"My dear," Sandy said, "you know I would have told you. But let me ask the barman." He turned. "Phillip, has there been a telephone call for Hob recently?"

"Nothing," Phillip said. "I would have said."

"Could I use the phone?" Hob asked. "It's sorta important."

Sandy had one of the few phones in Santa Eulalia at that time, and he didn't like to tie it up with customers. But Hob was a special case, and brought a certain panache to the island with his detective agency. "Of course. Just try not to tie it up too long. And be sure to get time and charges from the operator if you're calling off the island."

Hob went upstairs to the small tiled room where Sandy slept on nights when he kept the bar opened late and didn't want to drive all the way to his finca in Siesta. He got the Ibiza operator and put in a call to Nigel's present digs in Edna Schumacher's apartment. No answer. He tried to reach him at his small, entailed house in Kew Gardens, London, without success. Then he put in a call to the Kit Kat Bar in Paris where Jean-Claude was currently getting his phone calls. The proprietor said that Jean-Claude was out of town, he didn't know where, and could he take a message? Hob said who he was and stressed the importance of his reaching Jean-Claude immediately; couldn't the proprietor even make a guess as to his whereabouts? The proprietor said, "You may well be his employer, m'sieu, but for me you are only a voice on the telephone. But perhaps you know Jean-Claude. If so, you know he would kill me if I told you where he was. And anyhow, I swear to you, I do not know."

Hob remembered to get his time and charges for the call. When he came down, he asked Sandy to add them to his tab. Then, seeing Harry Hamm had just come in, he showed him Jean-Claude's note.

"You've always told me Nigel is absentminded," Harry said. "This is proof of it. Do you think Annabelle might know something?"

"She might," Hob said. "She's the only person I know who knows both Nigel and Señor Arranque. I'll take a run in and see."

"Want me to come?" Harry said. "I got nothing better to do."

They went to Ibiza in Harry's car, went around the city to Figueretas, and so to Annabelle's building, The Beehive, arriving at about ten in the evening. Annabelle's apartment was dark, and she didn't respond to repeated knocking. But her next-door neighbor, Dolores, came out in a bathrobe with a towel wrapped around her head.

"Are you Hob Draconian?" she asked.

When Hob said that he was, she said, "Annabelle thought you might come by. She left a note for you." She went in and got it and handed it to Hob.

The note read, "Hob, dear, something very important has come up, and I've left for London. With a little luck I'll be able to find out what you want to know. In case you decide to come, which might be a good idea, I'll be staying at Arlene's." There followed a South Kensington telephone number.

Back at the car, Hob sat for a moment, thinking. Harry waited, then finally asked, "So where to now?"

"Airport," Hob said.

"You haven't packed anything."

"I've got my passport, money, and address book. I'll pick up a razor and an extra pair of jeans in London."

# THREE

# LONDON

# 1

THE PLANE LEFT on time, and the flight was uneventful. The weather was overcast, but the Iberia plane got below the ceiling when it came in over Land's End. Soon the green and pleasant country of England was spread out below. They arrived at Heathrow just past noon.

After passing through customs and immigration, Hob took the airport bus to Victoria Station. He found a telephone booth and tried once more to call Nigel in Paris at Edna Schumacher's apartment. No answer. Just on the off chance, he telephoned Kew Gardens. There was no answer.

It was going on noon. Hob had lunch at a pizza place near Victoria, then made a few more phone calls, this time looking for a place to stay. None of the people he knew seemed to be in town. It looked as if he was going to have to spend money on accommodations, something he avoided on principle as well as out of practicality. He dug out his little brown imitation leather telephone book and found the telephone number of Lorne Atena, a West Indian artist he had met at a party in Paris. He telephoned. Lorne answered and told Hob he was welcome to stay as long as he didn't mind listening to steel band music and sleeping on the couch. Hob didn't much like either idea, but beggars can't be choosers, even if they are private detectives. He decided to try it out for a night, then see what else he could find.

Lorne's place was on Westbourne Grove in the heart of London's West Indian enclave. It was a long, wide, slightly seedy road noted for its antique shops and race riots. Lorne buzzed him through. His apartment was a fourth-floor walk-up. When Hob arrived, more than a little out of breath, Lorne greeted him effusively. Lorne was a light-skinned black who affected the dreadlocks of the Rastafarians because he thought they looked attractive on him. He was a saxophone player and a good one.

"Hey, man, good to see you. Come on in, drop the white man's burden." Lorne was a little man and he moved fast, darting around offering Hob a beer, a chicken sandwich, and one of the big West Indian joints rolled in newspaper and guaranteed to put you out for the rest of the day. Hob regretfully declined. He needed his wits, such as they were, about him for what he suspected was coming next.

Lorne gave him an extra key. Hob showered, shaved, and changed into fresh clothing that Lorne loaned him: jeans, a wool lumberjack's shirt, and a Freetown Tornados warm-up jacket. Then, sitting in Lorne's Victorian sitting room smoking a Ducado, he found George Wheaton's business number where he had scribbled it on a torn piece of paper, and telephoned.

George's secretary answered, asked him to wait, had a whispered conversation, then put him through to George. Hob started to introduce himself, but George remembered their meeting several years ago. Hob said he was looking for Nigel and said that it was urgent.

"I thought he was in Paris," George said.

"I thought he was in London, but I got a message he was in Paris. Now I don't know where he is, and it's important that I reach him."

"As a matter of fact," George said, "I've been looking for him myself. I don't know what to tell you. Have you tried stopping by Derek Posonby's gallery in the West End? You might have a look in there. When I call them, I always get put on hold. Tell you what. Why don't you come out to my house this evening, say around seven, and we'll put our heads together, see what we can come up with. I hope Nigel is not being a naughty boy again."

"I hope not, too," Hob said. He wrote down the address.

Next he tried to reach Annabelle at Arlene's London telephone number. Arlene answered and said Annabelle was out—shopping, she added unnecessarily—but she'd been hoping Hob would call. Could Annabelle call him back? Hob left Lorne's number and said he'd try again in a few hours.

He tried to reach Jean-Claude in Paris but got the same man as last night—and the same blank refusal to divulge anything about Jean-Claude's whereabouts.

Finally he telephoned Patrick, got his fiancée Anne-Laure, who told him that Patrick had gone to Amsterdam for a few days to visit friends.

"There was a letter for you, Hob," Anne-Laure said, "but Nigel came by last week and took it with him. It was sent express."

"How was it addressed?"

"To you, care of the agency, at this address."

"Nigel opened it and read it while you were there?"

"Yes."

"Did he tell you anything about what it said or who it was from?"

"No. He read it quickly, nodded, pursed his lips, said, 'Aha' in a way that might indicate the thought: 'isn't that interesting' or 'funny how things work out'—it was that sort of aha! And then he put the letter back in its envelope, put it in his pocket, thanked me, and left."

"How many pages was the letter?"

"One page. I'm pretty sure of that."

"Did the envelope have a return address?"

"I don't think so. But I really didn't notice."

"Was there anything unusual about the envelope or the letter that you remember? In appearance, I mean?"

"The paper crinkled when Nigel opened it. So it must have been good paper. Heavy. That's the sort that crinkles, isn't it?"

"I think so. Do you remember anything else about either the letter or envelope?"

"Just the crest on the letter."

"Crest? Are you sure?"

"No, I'm not sure. I'm searching through my memory, trying to come up with something that'll help, but for all I know I'm making it up. But I *think* there was a sort of raised circular seal or crest on the letter. It was yellow and red, I think."

Hob stopped himself from asking again, "Are you sure of that?" and said instead, "Was there a similar crest on the envelope?"

"I don't think so. No crest and no return address."

"Okay, you're doing fine. Now, is there anything else you can think of?"

"Just that Nigel asked if he could make a call on our phone."

"You said yes, of course?"

"Of course."

"And who did he call?"

"Hob, I don't have a clue. He asked me if I'd mind making him some coffee, so I went to the kitchen and made coffee, and when I got back he had finished his call and was off the phone and looking very pleased with himself."

"And then?"

"He said he had to call Jean-Claude."

"And what did he say to him?"

"He didn't get Jean-Claude, so he said he'd probably find him in one of the cafés near the Forum, and off he went."

"And that's it?"

"That's it. That's all I can remember. In fact, I'm afraid it's more than I really do remember."

# 2

NIGEL WAS FEELING optimistic and hopeful when he decided to go to the Caribbean island of San Isidro. His good mood began to dissolve as Europe faded behind the Flamingo 737, and the long featureless Atlantic formed up beneath him. It had suddenly occurred to Nigel that he really didn't want to be traveling at all. What Nigel really wanted to do was get back to London as quickly as possible. It was late June, getting close to his mother's birthday. Nigel and his brother, George, always went to mother's place, Druse Hall near Ayrshire in southern Scotland for her birthday. Nigel didn't like to miss these occasions. His mother was eighty-three this birthday. It was an important one for her. And though she made light of her years, Nigel knew that age and the fear of impending death weighed heavily on her. She had begun talking about Nigel's father again, Charles Francis Wheaton, who had been killed in Lebanon eight years ago, blown up in his jeep with two United Nations observers while covering a story for the *Guardian*. Charles and Hester had been separated for years and saw each other only on important family occasions. But something had gone out of Hester when Charles was killed. She only spoke of him when she felt her own end drawing near, when the arthritis was worse than usual, or when the heart palpitations started. Nigel had always been the black sheep of the family and the apple of Hester Wheaton's eye. George was a dull stick, safely entrenched in the civil service, where he held down some boring job in the Counterintelligence Section of MI5 and dithered about whether or not he should marry Emily, to whom he had been engaged unofficially for almost three years.

Nigel wanted to be there for Hester. So much of his life he had not been there for his family. Four years ago Hester had undergone a painful gallstone operation alone because Nigel had been in Chad trying to interview Sanj al-Attar during his brief employment by the Anti-Slavery Commission. There had been other occasions, other family crises, when Nigel had been absent. They weren't a closely knit family, the Wheatons, but they had a grim Scots loyalty, tight-lipped, dour, reliable. Nigel felt he was forever letting them down. He was the oldest. He considered himself the most worldly. He was good with his hands and loved nothing better than to get into old clothes and do some of the work that Druse Hall, his mother's estate, always required. Nigel enjoyed this work. He was especially interested in the stone fences. They were not especially old, only a century or two, but they were a fine example of the stonefitter's art. The stones had been selected with care, and in Scotland there is never a lack of stones to choose from, and fitted together so cunningly that you couldn't fit a knifeblade between them. Nigel hadn't seen better stonework anywhere in Europe, not even in Ibiza, where the older stone walls were put together as neatly as the Egyptian pyramids or the strange temples on Machu Picchu. And like them, the stone fences of Druse Hall had never been sullied with mortar.

Nigel loved well-shaped old stone things. He was a fair amateur architect, and had designed and built his own finca in Ibiza, near San Jose, just below Escabells. He had lost it, of course, in the divorce settlement. But he had a contract to rebuy it at a set price. If only he could get the money, which as the years wore on, seemed more and more dubious. His mother's house in Scotland was the nearest thing he had now to a home. He didn't consider the house in Kew a home. He had bought it during a period of temporary prosperity, mostly as an investment but also in order to have a place to stay while he was in England.

He had remodeled the interior, increasing its value considerably. It was on King Street, halfway between the underground station and the main entrance to Kew Gardens. A good location, a bit run-down at present, more so since the great storm that had devastated Kew, but a good investment still, one likely to show a profit if he ever chose to sell. Meanwhile he lived in a single basement room in the house because he had rented out the rest, the two apartments he had made on the ground floor and the three bedsitters he rented on the upper floors. It was a nice house, but Nigel had never really warmed to it. His heart was in stone, the living stone of Scotland and Ibiza, the mellow stone that spoke of time and tradition. Perhaps it was his love of old things, foreign things, that drove him on. It was a damnable itch, the taste for foreign faces and places, for the exotic places of the world, an itch that drove him forth again and again, and he was always missing important dates because of it, dates such as his mother's birthday.

The more he thought about it, the more huffy he became. The nerve of this Santos fellow, who probably thought Nigel was some sort of merchant peddler. He didn't want his bloody business, not even his bloody five hundred dollar retainer. He'd have to stay on the bloody island overnight, and even with the best connections he could not get to London before the day after tomorrow. He would miss his mother's birthday again, and that was insupportable.

It was in his mind to cancel, to hell with this, he'd go back home and be with his family. His sister, Alice, needed his support, too, though, reading between the lines of her angry story, it sounded as if her husband, Kyle, was more to be pitied. But Kyle had his own family to pity him, all those Joes and Bobs and T.C.s and Mary Jos whom Nigel had met briefly at Alice's wedding two and a half years ago in Dallas. Alice was a bit of a shrew, of course—in all fairness Nigel had to admit that—and her husband's worst crime against her seemed to have been leaving Alice alone a lot while he went about his business—wildcatting, the business that enabled Alice to live in style in the big farmhouse

187 miles south of Amarillo until she couldn't stand it anymore, though she ought to have known what she was getting into before she married Kyle. Still, she was Nigel's sister, part of his family, even if she and Nigel had never gotten along. And more important, there was Mother.

"Would you care for a refreshment, sir?"

Nigel looked up, startled. In his musings he had lost all sense of time and place. Now he found himself once again on a three-quarter-empty airplane droning its way across the Atlantic. A stewardess had spoken to him, trim, slim, busty, quite pretty, late twenties or early thirties if he didn't miss his guess. She had golden skin—Eurasian, perhaps, one of Nigel's favorite mixtures.

"Refreshment?" Nigel said. "You serve spirits, I believe?"

"Yes, sir. What would you like?"

"A scotch, water on the side. Glenlivet, if you have it. And a little advice, my dear."

"Advice, sir? On what?"

"I'd appreciate a suggestion for a birthday present for a lady of eighty-three who has everything."

"Let me think about it while I get your drink," the stewardess said.

She went back to the pantry and returned with Nigel's drink. She was a Barbados girl living now in London. She seemed as attracted to large, impressive, middle-aged Englishmen with tawny beards, bright blue eyes, and a tousled head of graying reddish blond curls as Nigel was to golden-skinned, bright-eyed, good-looking Eurasian girls. They discussed the question of Nigel's mother's birthday, and then other matters, since work was light on the mostly empty flight. By the time they reached San Isidro, they had arranged to meet in the market in San Isidro that evening. Esther had seen a nicely framed primitive painting of the San Isidro waterfront done by a local artist of considerable renown on the island. It might be just the thing.

It was early afternoon when the jet banked for its approach to San Isidro. Looking down, Nigel saw a low, skinny, tree-clad island, with the coast of Venezuela looming beyond it. Little puffy clouds dotted the horizon, and the sun was shining with that easy brilliance we have come to expect of it in the tropics. Nigel had quite recovered from his attack of conscience and was now looking forward to meeting Esther, and, after her, Santos.

# 3

NEXT MORNING NIGEL was up bright and early. The airline stewardess, was just leaving, trim in her uniform, ready for her flight back to London. She blew him a kiss at the hotel-room door.

The primitive painting hadn't been quite the thing. But he and Esther had had a good time strolling around, and after that there'd been dinner at San Isidro's best restaurant, The Bluebeard, and then drinks and dancing at the Congreso's Twilight Grotto. And then fun and games in the room afterward, and now Nigel had coffee and croissants sent up and busied himself in the shower, getting ready to let Santos know he was indeed here. Too bad Esther had to fly back on the morning flight. But he expected to see her again in London.

Refreshed and breakfasted, Nigel stepped out of the Congreso into Puerto San Isidro's main street. Tall palms lined the macadam road. At roadside stalls people were selling vegetables and tinned goods. There was the usual clutter of two-, three-, and four-wheeled transportation. The usual Caribbean mixture of squalor, color, and good spirits.

Basically, local color aside, San Isidro was a depressing sight. The only thing it could be was a tropical paradise. It was obviously unsuited for any other role. Since there is little need for a tropical paradise in the modern world, San Isidro was a place looking for a product.

In the tin-roofed little town there were only a few good buildings. One with a gambrel roof, Dutch, to judge by its proportions.

"Dat is de bank, Sor," the bald taxi driver told him, in the chichi accent that is expected of taxi drivers in the Caribbean. "And over there, the Ramerie, where Morgan the pirate lived when he was made governor."

"Nice," Nigel said. "And what's this?" he asked, noticing a rather good example just up the street of Caribbean Georgian, a double-winged place with central entranceway, pillared at the base and with a veranda running the length of the upstairs. Fine old trees dotted the well-kept lawn.

"Dis de Government House, sor."

"Ah," said Nigel, brightening. "Take me up to the main entrance."

A smiling majordomo seemed to know who Nigel was as soon as he gave his name. He was led inside and up an impressive double staircase to an upstairs audience room all purple drapes and overstuffed furniture. Tall French windows were a nice feature. But several of them were boarded up. The room was impressive, but it hadn't been swept recently.

If Santos had been expecting Hob, he showed no signs of disappointment when Nigel Wheaton presented himself instead. Santos came bustling out of a side office, a small brown-skinned man with a little pointed beard and clear resemblance to Robert de Niro in his role of Mr. Cyphre in *Angelheart*. Santos was wearing a nicely tailored tropical-weight white suit and pointed tan shoes. He wore several decorations, and he greeted Nigel with a strong, two-handed handshake.

"I am delighted to meet you, Major Wheaton. I only wish Mr. Draconian had been able to come as well."

"Hob sends his regrets. An unavoidable press of work prevented his accepting your kind invitation. He sends his best wishes."

"I am so glad he was able to spare you, Major."

"For a day or two only, alas. The agency is flooded with work."

"As well it should be," Santos said. "Well, since our time is limited, why don't we get right down to it? But first, please accept this." He pressed a folded check into Nigel's hand. "And of course the hotel has been instructed to send your bill directly to me."

"You are too kind," Nigel said, just remembering that he had seen a very nice looking silver service in the gift shop within the hotel arcade. It might be just the thing for an old lady's eighty-third birthday.

Santos took him on a tour of Government House, pointing out the many objets d'art the place boasted. There were rows of expensive period furniture, drapes, and wall hangings from great eras in European history and endless glass cases filled with what Santos referred to as "art treasures."

"This is a nice piece," Nigel said, indicating a small graceful bronze figure of a boy mounted on a dolphin.

"Sarzano," Santos said. "Let me show you some more."

He led Nigel down a long gloomy hallway. Portraits occupied the upper portions, each dimly lit by its own individual lamp that cast a yellowish glow over the faded oils. The corridor was a long one, a hundred feet at least. Lined up below the paintings were glass-topped cabinets, and within them were a variety of objects, all neatly tagged. There was a collection of Fabergé eggs whose value Nigel estimated at perhaps fifty thousand pounds. There was quite a lot of jewelry, its value difficult for Nigel to judge but of historic interest at least, bound to be valuable. One case was entirely given over to a display of Carthaginian coins. They appeared to be gold. It was difficult to estimate their value, but it had to be better than a hundred thousand pounds.

As he walked, Nigel kept a tab in his head. When he had reached a million pounds at lowest estimates, he stopped.

"Señor Santos, this is indeed a remarkable collection. I suppose you know it is quite valuable."

"I am not an expert on these matters," Santos said. "But I have always believed so, yes."

"How on earth did you get so many interesting objects together under one roof?"

"Oh, it is not *my* collection," Santos said. "Not my own personal collection, that is. What you are looking at is the official San

Isidran national heritage, which is in my care for the nation. What you see on these walls, in these cases. And there is more in the cellars, a lot of it still unpacked."

"Who put all this together?" Nigel asked.

"It has grown over the last two hundred years," Santos said. "San Isidro has had various rulers, and most of them contributed their bit. Then there were the pirates. Some of them became governors of our island. They, too, contributed many of these items, which at the time were of no great value, but have grown so over the years."

"It is a brilliant collection," Nigel said. "Am I correct in assuming that you are interested in selling some pieces?"

"Perfectly correct."

"And that, in fact, is what you wanted to see the Alternative Detective Agency about?"

"That is right," Santos said. "I might add, lest there be any misunderstanding, that I do not sell these objects for the purpose of personal enrichment. I am modestly wealthy, and what I have suits me very well. It is my poor country I am thinking of."

"Of course," Nigel said, trying to keep an ironic tone out of his voice.

But Santos appeared to be in earnest. He went on, "We have no product to sell to the outside world, no natural resources like oil or minerals, not even a strong tourist industry, since the beauties of our island, though considerable, are not the equal of Jamaica or the Bahamas. With the money I hope to realize from these treasures, I want to set up training schools and colleges for our local population."

"Which ones are you interested in selling, if I may ask?"

"Why, as for that," Santos said, with a negligent wave of the hand, "I would like to dispose of all or most of them, or at least the ones of greatest value."

Nigel made a flying guess as to the value of the entire collection. If what was in the other rooms was up to the standard of what he had seen, and if there was, say, twice as much stored away below as appeared here on the surface, the collection might be worth ten million pounds? Twenty million?

Nigel had the sudden feeling of a child who has stumbled into the house made of candy. "Take what you wish!" the old witch tells him. "They're all for you, my dearie." And he stuffs himself full. But when it comes time to leave . . . It was all simply too good.

"You have been a kind host," Nigel said. "I think it is only proper that I advise you as to proper procedure. You should contact one of the big galleries, Christie's in London, say, or Parke-Bernet in New York. Send them a catalog of what is here, with brief descriptions—and photographs, if possible. Ask them to send an appraiser. This is how these matters are commonly conducted."

"Could you not appraise the items for me?" Santos asked.

"I could have a go at it, but I am not an expert on these matters," Nigel said.

"But you work for a group of art dealers?"

"I do a little work in the field from time to time. But I repeat, I'm not an expert."

"These experts from Christie's," Santos said, "I suppose there would be a lot of publicity attendant upon their coming here?"

"It could be handled discreetly," Nigel said. "But Christie's would want an established provenance for all the objects. So they could announce them properly in their catalog, you see."

"Yes, it is as I thought," Santos said. "But you see, any sale of these objects must be handled with discretion."

"The big houses are the soul of discretion."

"But it might try their patience if I pointed out the procedure we had to go through to get these objects to market. You see, Mr. Wheaton, I must not appear to be selling these items. They are not mine. They belong to the nation. I am their caretaker, but not their owner."

"You have the right to sell them, however," Nigel pointed out.

"Let's not say the right. That's a matter for the law to decide. Let's say that I have the opportunity to sell them to provide something better for my people. They need new fishing boats more than they need old European masters. They need education into modern farming techniques more than they need a case of Venetian glass. They need a casino that will bring in tourists more than they need Fabergé eggs behind a glass case."

"I take your point," Nigel said.

"If I were to ask you to sell one of these objects for me," Santos said, "how would you proceed?"

"With or without papers?"

"Without, let us say. Is that uncommon?"

"Not at all. People walk into art dealers every day with items. No one knows where they came from. Some art dealers aren't too scrupulous about provenance. Not a major house like Christie's, of course."

"Do you know such houses?"

"In fact," Nigel said, "I do. But I assure you, Mr. Santos, if you can properly document what you sell, you would stand to realize a much greater profit on it."

"There is a difficulty about that," Santos said.

"I rather thought there might be," Nigel said.

"These pieces are part of the San Isidran national treasure. They have been amassed over the centuries for the enjoyment of the San Isidran people, of whom not more than five or ten a year come to look at their heritage. Much greater good could be done for the people if it were possible to sell these objects, and apply the income to public projects and the creation of new jobs."

"No doubt," Nigel said. "It is a lofty ambition. Might I ask, Señor Santos, if you are suggesting the theft of these objects? I don't mean to be insulting, but the transaction you are suggesting seems hardly straightforward."

"It is not exactly theft," Santos said. "But it is not exactly straightforward, either."

"And you thought the Alternative Detective Agency would be interested in a situation like this?"

"Yes, that is what I thought," Santos said. "I got the impression while dealing with Mr. Draconian that you were people to be trusted, that you were ethical, but that you were not interested in the exact letter of the law."

"Isn't that a contradiction?" Nigel asked.

"A true morality must exist in contradiction," Santos said.

"Interesting," Nigel said. "Let me pursue my question. Here we are in Government House, and here are these treasures. There are guards at the door. The treasure is not yours, by your own admission."

"Not mine," Santos agreed. "But I can take what I please."

"By thievery," Nigel said.

Santos smiled painfully. "The art treasures here are the heritage of the San Isidran people. I, however, am the President of San Isidro."

Nigel looked at him sharply to see if he was serious. He seemed to be.

"Are you indeed?" Nigel said.

"I assure you," Santos said, "I am."

"Why, one might ask, did you not mention this situation in your letter?"

"I wanted you to see what we had first. I wanted to appraise you while you appraised the goods. I am satisfied, and I hope you are. Perhaps we could take a glass of sherry in the Audience Room and continue our discussion?"

Nigel agreed. His mind was racing furiously. It was possible that Santos was selling him a line of goods, and that his real intention was to simply take the San Isidran people for whatever they were worth. On the other hand, Nigel's reading of the man was that he was sincere. The idea of a national patrimony was a sick sort of joke, anyhow—like giving people a mansion in which to starve or a great view in which to perish of thirst. Or a glorious death in terms of an abstraction.

"Now, about these goods," Nigel said. "If I understand the position correctly, you want to take some things out without people knowing it, in order to sell them in international markets."

"Yes, that sums it up pretty well," Santos said. "You understand I am doing this for the national good. We are a very small nation, Major Wheaton. We have the dubious pleasure of possessing the worst weather in the Caribbean. We have no industry, no resources. You may think, Major Wheaton, that this is a cynical scheme to rob the people of their heritage. But I will assure you that ninety cents on the dollar will go directly to the as-sistance of my people."

"Not that anyone is going to be standing over you checking the accounting," Nigel said, annoyed now.

"I have taken the trouble," Santos said, "to learn a little about your background, Major Wheaton. I believe you had a little trou-ble in Istanbul."

Nigel stared at him. "What the hell do you know about that?"

"Smuggling, wasn't it?"

Nigel knew he was under attack. He sat down, calm, com-posed, prepared to defend himself. Nigel never lost confidence, but he was aware that he seemed to have gotten himself into some sort of ugly set piece. It was strange and unsettling to find himself in this out-of-the-way corner of the world, in a big gloomy mansion, being badgered by this small Latin gentleman. It made Nigel realize once again how small the world was—and how sit-uations kept repeating themselves. He thought, not for the first time, how the whole idea of multiplicity was erroneous. Life was a play in which people only pretended to be strangers. Actually they knew one another very well. And there was no escaping them. "I walked the streets of the City of Ignorance looking for a stranger's face." He had read that line in a story by the American writer O. Henry, and it had stuck to him ever since.

"I suppose you've got my attendance records from Balliol, too," Nigel said. "And I assume, since you know everything else, you know I read history."

"But didn't take a degree," Santos said. "Would you like to hear your marital history?"

"No, thank you," Nigel said, "I know it only too well. You must have an efficient agency to collect all this for you so quickly."

"You would know that better than I," Santos said. "We worked with the Alternative Detective Agency. One of your sometime employers I believe, eh, Major Wheaton?"

"I'm no longer in service," Nigel said, shaken. "Plain mister will do nicely. Sent you my dossier, did they?"

"Not at all, Major. The facts about you were easy enough to dig out."

So he said. But Nigel wondered. That old suspicion, stronger than love, for Nigel, that love that continued to vote for death, all of that rose in Nigel's throat again. Istanbul. The bloody bad luck of it all. Or the cunning of it, if Hob had sold him out to Captain Kermak, as Jean-Claude suggested. The arrest, the trial, him and Jean-Claude led off to the pokey and released nine days later. Not much time to serve. But enough to get your name on the Interpol computer. Enough to get you stopped and searched and hassled at every checkpoint, until George brought enough pressure to bear to clear Nigel's name from the computer records because he had been arrested but never charged, and obviously never convicted. By rights he didn't belong on the database of known smugglers. But somehow his name stuck there for a long time. And with his criminal record he could never get a visa for the United States, could never live in New York—the city he had convinced himself, though he had never been able to visit it, was the epitome of the modern world, the city that would dominate the twenty-first century. There were ways to smuggle yourself into America, but then there was always the danger he'd be caught someday and shipped out, and all the work and time he'd have spent in New York would be in vain. He owed that one to Hob, too. If Hob had informed upon him. Which, of course, he still maintained Hob had not.

"I just wanted to make everything clear," Santos said. "Would you be willing to take on this work? On the understanding, of course, that Mr. Draconian is a full participant in this arrangement? We would find it a serious breach requiring action if Mr. Draconian, whom we respect, were somehow excluded."

"There's no problem about that," Nigel said stiffly, smiling but thinking unspeakable thoughts. He was wondering, Who put him on to the agency? Who does he know who knows Hob and me? Did Hob send him my dossier? What bloody game *is* this?

Santos made a room available for him. Nigel telephoned Jean-Claude in Paris and spoke to him about the importation of a considerable amount of art treasures, these to bypass customs and immigration. Jean-Claude said to send them to the port of

Cherbourg; he had friends there, and for the right consideration they'd be prepared to look the other way.

"I'll just need to make a selection," Nigel told Santos. "Your people will take care of the packing and shipping."

"That will be fine."

"I'll sell your items in Paris and remit the total to you less ten percent agents' fee. For the agency."

"That will be quite satisfactory. And I have something else that might interest you," Santos said. "It is a job. It involves helping a certain party buy art. European paintings. It would require your return to London immediately."

"No problem," Nigel said. "Let's hear about it."

# 4

HOB LEFT LORNE'S and took the underground to the Burlingame Arcade in the West End, where he went to Posonby's Gallery. Posonby's was all bright wood and indirect lighting and clever paintings. There were also several very large crystal ashtrays, but they were so highly polished that Hob decided not to desecrate them by filling them with cigarette butts. Derek Posonby was of medium height, plump, with a round face and round, gold-rimmed glasses. He was wearing what Hob supposed was an Edwardian suit, gray with a discreet stripe, and he wore highly polished black cordovan pumps. His thinning hair was combed over to cover his scalp. In compensation, perhaps, he had grown his sideburns long and fluffy. It made his round, somewhat raw face look like an egg hatching from a nest of hair. Derek had an ingenuous look; he peered around like a bird looking for a crumb. He looked soft and easy to take. This was a big help in the art business, where inoffensive appearance and mild manner can translate into substantial markups.

"What do you want Nigel for?" Derek asked after Hob asked.

"I've got a job for him," Hob said. "The agency needs his talents."

"He might not take you up on it," Derek said. "You know Nigel. Put twenty quid in his pocket and he forgets all about working until it's gone. Last of the flower children, is our Nigel."

"He was working for you recently, wasn't he?" Hob asked.

"Oh, he flogged off the odd piece of art for us now and then," Derek said.

"I believe he did a job for you recently," Hob said.

"Yes, he did. But that sort of thing is confidential. Trade secrets and all that, you know."

"Look," Hob said, "I really need to know exactly what went on. I'm afraid Nigel is mixed up in something. It's caught the attention of the Paris police. I'm conducting this investigation on their behalf."

Derek didn't like it. He made a great thing of his professionalism, but he was as dotty as half the art dealers in London. Twisted bunch of people, in Hob's opinion, but Derek wasn't a bad sort. Quite a fine art knowledge, especially sound on fourteenth-century Dutch and French masters. Not that he saw many of them. He was no less honest than any of that breed. After all, a picture's worth is pretty subjective. It's worth what the dealer thinks he can get for it. Derek didn't want to talk about how he was doing, but of course he did want to talk about it, because that's all that bunch of dealers did, meet in Squire's Coffee Shop on the King's Road and brag about who they did that week. That's exaggerating slightly, but nothing stays a secret in the London art world very long. One big pack of squabbling Janes. So it didn't take much coaxing on Hob's part for Derek to come out with the story. In fact, once he started, he got quite enthusiastic about it, even called in young Christopher, who had been there when Nigel performed his remarkable coup. And so, with Derek's voice rising and falling, and the fans turning, young Christopher took up the tale.

"I want to buy paintings," the dark-haired South American man said. "I am Arranque."

He was a medium-sized, burly, dark, black-haired man in a chamois western-cut sports jacket that looked as if it could have cost more than his first-class plane fare from Caracas. It was difficult for the salespeople in Posonby's to get an impression of the man because all eyes were on the sports coat. The coat was all the more remarkable in that it was one of the earliest appearances of fawn-and-mauve men's clothing in London; its first appearance, in fact, since the days of Thomas the Tailor, as told in the newly discovered text addenda to Chaucer's Canterbury Tales.

The man himself was worth noticing, however, immediately after the coat, since the man had presumably bought the coat and therefore had access to top tailoring. Arranque had a broad, glowering face set off by a small mustache. He wore boots made from the skins of an extinct species of reptile. An emerald glittered on his finger, just below the popped knuckle. He brought a breath of refreshing vulgarity to the dark and proper art gallery.

His first words, addressed to Christopher, the nervous young clerk who inquired as to his wishes, were, again, "I want to buy paintings."

"Yes, sir," said Christopher. "What kind of paintings, sir?"

"That is secondary. What I need is fifty-five yards' worth of paintings."

Christopher's lower jaw dropped in a really theatrical gawp. "I'm afraid we don't sell paintings by the yard, sir. Not in Posonby's."

"What do you mean?" Arranque said.

"A painting, sir, you see, is a qualitative thing and therefore . . . "

Nigel came rushing in just then. He was just back from San Isidro, had just bused in from the airport. He dropped his light suitcase near the door and strode in majestically.

"That will be all, Christopher," Nigel said. "I will look after Señor Arranque personally."

"Yes, sir," Christopher said. "Thank you, sir," he added, as he realized that he had almost killed a sale and had therefore jeopardized his own job.

"Señor Arranque?" Nigel said. "I am sorry to be late. My plane just arrived. May I give you some coffee?"

Nigel escorted Arranque to Derek's office. He made sure the client was comfortably seated. Luckily enough Derek's thirty-year-old port was in its usual position, and the box of Havanas was where it was supposed to be. He sent Christopher out for coffee and adjusted the big Italian ceramic ashtray on Derek's desk until it was just to his liking.

"Now, sir," Nigel said, "let me just be clear about this. All Mr. Santos told me was that you were seeking to acquire a group of paintings in a hurry. He did not go into specifics. Might I inquire as to what you require?"

"I am glad you get straight to the point," Arranque said. "I need exactly fifty-five yards of paintings for my new hotel, and I need them almost immediately." He made an imperious gesture with his right hand.

"Quite," Nigel said. "Let me just be sure I understand the position. Are you seeking to purchase paintings in the *length* of fifty-five yards, or do you want paintings whose combined *area* equals fifty-five square yards?"

"No, I mean the first, the length," Arranque said. "I have fifty-five yards of hallway to cover, and I want paintings on them. Not squeezed together tight, but spaced let's say a couple of inches apart. How many paintings would I need to cover fifty-five yards?"

"Depends," Nigel said. "Is that fifty-five yards to one leg of the corridor, or have you doubled the length to have pictures on both legs?"

"I've doubled them, of course. What do you take me for?"

"I just wanted to make sure we were both talking about the same thing. You'd want these pictures framed, of course?"

"Of course."

Nigel made a meaningless squiggle on a scratch pad he found on Derek's desk. "And spaced apart?"

"Spaced apart a few inches, I should think," Arranque said. "Though I'm no expert in these matters."

"But your instincts are perfectly sound," Nigel said. "Let's see." He found pencil and paper and began to make calculations. "Let's say we put up one oil painting not to exceed two feet in width in every yard space. That would allow space between them and come to approximately fifty-five paintings, though you might want a few more just to be on the safe side."

"Fifty-five paintings for fifty-five yards. Yes, that sounds right," Arranque said.

Nigel wrote down figures. "You're quite sure it's fifty-five yards? Shame to get the paintings all the way back to South America and find you've undercalculated."

"Fifty-five yards," Arranque said. "I walked off the distance myself. And they're going to my new hotel in Ibiza."

Nigel raised an eyebrow but didn't comment. "Did you take into account both sides of the corridors?"

Arranque's face screwed up and he snarled an oath in Spanish that was old when Simon Bolivar was still a babe in swaddling clothes. "You're right, I forgot to count both sides! You have good grasp, señor."

Nigel replied in his graceful Spanish, employing the complimentary mode. Then he got back to business. "And does this number include paintings for the individual rooms?"

"¡Caramba! I forgot that, too. There are two hundred and twelve rooms. Each room will need two paintings, one for the bedroom and one for the sitting room."

"Yes, that would be the minimum," Nigel said. "All right, that adds up to four hundred and twenty-four paintings just for the rooms. Agreed?"

Arranque nodded.

"So we have now a total of five hundred thirty-four paintings, then. If they are no more than two feet wide."

"How much will it cost?"

Nigel said, "That depends, of course, Señor Arranque. As you are no doubt aware, paintings differ greatly in price."

"I am aware of that," Arranque said. "I also know one can buy indifferent framed copies for as low as ten or twenty dollars a painting. I have seen such things in the big department stores in Caracas. But I don't want that. I pretend to no knowledge in this regard, but I do have my criteria. I want all my paintings to be originals by European artists whose names appear in at least two reliable art books. They needn't be famous, but they should be recognized as being of merit, or whatever it is second-rate painters are noted for. Everything must be correct in my new hotel. I must also have the reference books and be able to show the names to any who may be skeptical."

"A sound way. Experts are paid to be right."

"I am prepared to pay fifty thousand dollars for this if the paintings meet my standards."

Nigel nodded and decided to take the plunge. "Frankly, that's a little low, I'm afraid."

Arranque looked annoyed. "I'm not going to sit here and bargain like a peasant in the marketplace. I'll go to one hundred thousand, but not one cent more. And the paintings must be delivered to my hotel in Ibiza immediately, where I will look them over. If I feel they are suitable for my hotel, I will purchase them immediately."

"And if not?"

"Then you can take them back to London."

Nigel shook his head. "If you should decline to purchase them, our pictures will have been off the market for a period of time when they could have been sold. And we will also be out our insurance costs, freighting, air fares, and so on."

"I will pay two thousand dollars deposit on my purchase," Arranque said. "Or pounds, if you prefer. If I fail to buy, the money will reimburse you your time and expenses."

"That seems all right," Nigel said. England in general, and Europe in particular, was filled with oils by painters whose names could be found in at least two standard reference books, available at Posonby's, and whose vile daubings could be bought from ten pounds and up—but not too far up in most cases. Posonby stood to make a nice profit from this.

Arranque stood up. "Mr. Wheaton, something about you tells me you have been a military man."

Nigel smiled negligently. "Still shows, does it? Doesn't mean a damn thing, old boy. I'm a civvie now."

"I feel a bond between us. Will you pick out my paintings personally?"

"It will be my pleasure," Nigel said, thinking of several Glucks he could buy for about fifteen pounds a square yard, and a couple of Meyerbeers for even less.

"And bring them yourself and arrange to have them hung. I have confidence in you."

Nigel had heard that before. People had confidence in him. But that didn't make him a confidence man. At least, he hoped not. He was going to make plenty of money for Hob and the agency on the Santos deal; who could begrudge him this amusing little extra windfall?

"And then?" Hob asked.

"Then he accompanied the paintings to Ibiza," Derek said. "We crated them up and he accompanied the truck to Southhampton. Took the boat to Bilbao and Gibraltar and then to Ibiza. I suppose they should be arriving just about now. All legal, of course. It was a bit of a calculated risk. We didn't know if Arranque was doped up or crazy when he made that purchase. Nigel should have secured his check in advance. If that were possible. As it is, we almost stopped the deal. Too chancy. But Nigel insisted he could handle it, and so we sent him off with the paintings. Didn't we, Christopher?"

"Indeed we did, sir," Christopher said, pushing back the shock of blond hair from his eyes. "He even insisted on a new wardrobe."

"In case he calls around," Derek said, "how can he get in touch with you?"

Hob felt that exasperation he so often felt when dealing with Nigel's vagaries. But there seemed to be a goodly amount of money involved for the agency, and that was all to the good. He just hoped Nigel knew what he was doing. Nigel didn't, often. Hob gave Derek the address and telephone number of his friend Lorne in Westbourne Grove and left.

It was midafternoon. Too early to catch a train out to see George. What do detectives do between leads when they're on a case? Hob went to Piccadilly and saw an American detective movie. It was something with a lot of action in it, and it starred people who looked familiar to Hob, though he wasn't sure what they were famous for. The detective in this one had a lot of trouble because women kept throwing themselves at him, getting in his way just when he was close to solving the case. Hob had never had that sort of trouble with women. He also didn't usually get shot at as often as this detective in the movie did. Aside from that, they'd gotten it pretty right.

By the time the movie was over it was time for Hob to head out to George's house.

# 5

THE TOWN OF Fredmere Burton was about forty miles due north of London in Buckinghamshire. It was picturesque. Hob hadn't come there to sightsee, however. He was there to talk to George Wheaton.

George Wheaton was Nigel's younger brother, the one who did something or other in Intelligence. Nigel had never said much about George, except to lament his inability to form a good love relationship, which, according to Nigel, was the most important thing in the world, though his own record in this regard was dubious to say the least.

For the last seven years George had been keeping company with Emily Barnes, his neighbor in Fredmere Burton. She (and her bedridden mother) lived in the next semidetached house on Lancashire Row, the house beside George's. It wasn't at all a suitable house for George. He had inherited it and had moved in because it was convenient to the Ministry of Defence, which had recently been relocated to north London.

Emily was pretty in a faded way, dressed expensively without much style, was usually cheerful but not stupidly so, and had a good sense of humor. She worked at something technical in the Air Ministry. She was much sought after, in a quiet sort of way, and used to have quite a few dates. One month she had lunch in the Last Chance Saloon on Gloucester Road near Old Brompton on four separate occasions, each time with a different young man. It is not recorded what she thought of the rather dubious enchilladas served by that pretenious hamburger palace with its cutesy American-style advertising.

Emily was certainly not loose in her behavior. Sensible, that's what people called her. She had a nervous habit of ducking her head when spoken to abruptly, something to do with an experience in Scotland when she was eleven. Quite an odd story. But nothing to do with what was going on, because it was George who was brother to the dear ne'er-do-well Nigel, and therefore it was George that Hob went to with the photograph.

George was outside gardening. Very little grew in his garden, partly because of the overhanging trees, which couldn't be cut because lindens were rare in those parts and also because the sun, for reasons best known to itself, during its rare appearances in Buckinghamshire chose to duck behind clouds just when it could have shone over Songways, as George's cottage had been named by the last parson of Little Kenmore, the village about four miles from George's cottage in Fredmere Burton.

The small cottage was typical of the old building style in those parts, with its high-peaked roof of warple tied together with straw inswitches, nearly a lost art in England these days when every lad wanted to go to London and play in a rock band instead of apprenticing to the mind-bogglingly dull and badly-paying crafts of the past. It was almost certain that binding the warple with inswitches would become no more than a memory within the next ten or so years, since the last master of that art, Rufus Blackheen, was now eighty-five years old and bedridden, may God be merciful to his oddly mixed nature. George was not unmoved by the loss of this traditional industry, but though feeling almost everything keenly, he was too inhibited to express anything by changes in his outer demeanor. But by the pained expression on his face, and the suppressed winces with which he responded to leading questions on matters of special concern to him despite his effort to preserve an unmoved countenenance, it was obvious how he felt, since the very contours of his inwardness became a bas relief sort of thing, the details of which by their very smallness telegraphed their absolute and implacable bigness. That George was aware of these matters was evident by the nervous twitch of self-consciousness with which he greeted Hob at his cottage door.

"Oh, er, how do you do," George said. "You must be Hob, Nigel's friend. I believe we met once very briefly at my mother's birthday party some five years ago."

"We did meet on that occasion," Hob said, "and it was my very great pleasure to make the acquaintance of both you and your mother. I thought she was one classy dame, if you'll pardon the Americanism."

"No offense taken. Do come in, Hob. Do you take tea? Or would you prefer a beer? Or a real drink? Gin?"

"Tea would be fine," Hob said, since it was the closest he was apt to come to coffee. Not that coffee wasn't served in many private homes in England, to say nothing of most restaurants, which of course will serve anything as long as it makes a profit. But all too often it was instant coffee, which the English took to with an alacrity that belied their well-known good taste and intelligence. But we shall say no more on this matter.

George led Hob inside. Hob found himself in a small, dark living room crowded with tables covered with china cats, and with antiques of many other kinds scattered around the room and masquerading as chairs, couches, chaise longues, and the like. It was a pleasantly English sort of room. That was the first thing that occurred to Hob upon entering it. How English it was, with George walking tall and thin and stoop shouldered ahead of him and the inevitable starling poking a beady eye into the window and an artificial coal fire burning in the grate, or perhaps a real one—it didn't matter; they both looked the same. George led Hob into the little kitchen, with the gingham curtains and the Toby mugs and the other typically English objects, and put up the kettle and did the other things necessary to produce a cup, actually two cups, of tea in the English manner.

George was a good sort, but he had none of the electricity of Nigel. And yet you could see a resemblance in the brothers. Like so many of us, they were each a little potty in a way characteristic of their family. Mrs. Wheaton, their mother, was potty, too, but in such a commanding manner that she was frequently asked to speak at women's clubs and friends of the library groups on the Importance of Conviction in an Age Without Values.

"I've been wanting to get in touch with you, Hob. I was going to ask Nigel for your address, but he's been out of touch for quite a while."

"I know," Hob said. "I was hoping you might be able to tell me how to find him."

"Oh, dear," George said. "I had been hoping the same of you. Cream or lemon?"

"Bit of both, I imagine," Hob said. "No, wait, I was thinking of Nigel, not the tea."

"I thought perhaps that was what you meant," George said, the faintness of his tone indicating his desire not to give offense. He poured the tea (which had come to a boil and steeped as quickly as it did due to a new process that George, a civil servant whose hobby was inventing, had perfected only last year but had not gotten around to offering to lease or sell to the tea companies through sheer but rather lovable diffidence). Hob added his own sugar, and took lemon rather than cream.

Since George was interested, and worried about his brother, Hob brought him up to date on this latest investigation of the Alternative Detective Agency. He told him about Stanley Bower in Paris; the man with the emerald ring; his own search in Ibiza for who had seen Bower last; his warning from the South American heavies; his receipt of a money order from Jean-Claude, telling him about a case that Nigel was working on, but not going into details, his inability since then to get in touch with either Jean-Claude or Nigel to clear the matter up, his coming to London; and his plan to see Annabelle.

It had been going on six weeks since George had last seen his brother. Nigel's mood at that time had not been good. Since both George and Hob were aware of the depressing effect of the loss of his investment in the Mauritanian weapons venture had on Nigel, they didn't have to dwell on it. And George also knew, as apparently did half of London, about Nigel's recently successful flogging off of a bunch of mediocre though absolutely genuine

European paintings of no great skill, visual appeal, or lineage to an untutored but intuitive (in this case wrongly so) Venezuelan drug dealer. What came after that was more than a little unclear. Nigel had returned to Ibiza, that much was certain, because he had telephoned his brother from Brussels a few days ago. "Can't talk right now, old boy. Tell Mum I'm absolutely not going to miss her next birthday, and I've brought something special for her. I'll see you both in a few days.

"And since then?" Hob asked.

"Nothing." George hesitated a moment, then said, "Hob, if it would not be out of line, I'd like to offer a word or two of advice. I know that's frightfully impudent of me, but as you know I work in government, and my sector, insignificant though it is, gets word of goings-on from time to time. Hob, from what you tell me, you're getting in over your head. This matter of soma is potentially serious, and very dangerous. I beg you to watch yourself."

"I'm trying to do just that," Hob said. "What is bothering me right now is what Nigel is doing in all this. He seems to be working for the man I suspect of killing Stanley Bower. He also seems to have not a clue of what might really be going on."

"That bothers me, too, Hob," George said. "I'll redouble my efforts to find Nigel. And when you do reach him, or he you, please let me know at once, will you not? I'd also like to know when you hear from Jean-Claude."

Hob promised to be in touch as soon as he knew anything from anyone, and left.

After Hob was gone, George called his chief of operations on the special phone reserved for emergencies. The phone lines were working for a change, and he got through at once. He could picture the long, low room, lit by fluorescents overhead, with its rows of cubbyholes and tiny offices and its second tier of senior personnel upstairs. That's where the chief would be.

"Who's it this time?" the chief asked crossly.

"It's me," George said, cautious as always.

"Oh. Is this who I think it is?"

"I think so."

"George?"

"I'd rather you didn't use my name over the line."

"It's a secure line."

"There are no really secure lines."

"I suppose not," the chief grumbled. "Well, if you don't want to talk to me, what do you want?"

"I do want to talk to you," George said. "I suppose I'm being overcautious." He cleared his throat. "It's about the soma group we're keeping track of for Future Developments, sir. You've received the recent data I sent you from New York and Paris?"

"Yes, of course. Damned interesting. We've taken note of it. Has something else come through?"

"As a matter of fact, it has. These soma people are going into full-scale operation very soon. Several more people are implicated, though only marginally."

"Why tell me all this, George? You could have sent it in your weekly minute."

"I know, sir. But in this case, I thought some immediate action was necessary."

"Did I hear you right? George, you know very well that our Future Developments division is purely information collecting and advisery. Our charter strictly prohibits us from engaging in any action whatsoever."

"I realize that, sir. As you will remember, I helped draw up the charter guidelines. It was the only way government would let us operate at all."

"Well, then?"

"The situation at the moment is somewhat different. This soma matter is about to begin in a big way."

"Well, I suppose you could drop an anonymous word to the relevant police authorities."

"No, sir. I want to take a more direct step."

"A *direct* step? George, have you gone mad?"

"I hope not, sir. But the fact is, I have family involved in this soma matter. My brother, Nigel, to be precise. Inadvertently on his part, but involved nonetheless. His employer, the Alternative Detective Agency, is about to get into serious trouble, and that will involve Nigel. I need to take some steps over that."

"I quite understand your feelings," the chief said. He knew Nigel, too, and liked him. "But I'm afraid I cannot authorize it."

"The action I contemplate is quite small, sir. Almost innocuous."

"George, I'm going to tell you again what you very well know. Future Developments is allowed to operate only on a rule of absolute noninterference. We watch. And we advise. But we do nothing else. Sometimes the heart longs for action. Especially when those near and dear to us are involved. But it cannot be. Do you understand?"

"Yes, sir."

"But do you really understand?"

"Yes, sir. Thank you for your time."

Once he was off the phone, George unlocked the bottom drawer of his desk and took out a small book filled with indecipherable jottings and numbers. He had memorized the code long ago, so he had no trouble finding the number he was looking for and dialing it. He hummed softly to himself as he waited for a connect. He was glad he had this understanding with the chief. The phrase "Do you really understand?" coming after the phrase "Do you understand?" was George's go-ahead signal. And the beauty of it was, no one would ever know the chief had given his okay in the unlikely event that their scrambled telephone line proved to be not sufficiently scrambled after all.

After making his call, George walked up and down for a while and at last made himself another cup of tea. Finally he remembered with a start and opened the door to the attic. Emily came down the stairs. She was wearing a tartan jumper over a black skirt and white blouse. She had on lizard-skin shoes of darkest red.

"Sorry about that," George said. "I thought it was best he didn't see you here."

"Who was that?"

"Oh, some friend of Nigel's," George said.

There was no reason not to give Hob's name. But habits of security die hard.

# 6

THE TRAIN FROM Burton brought Hob to Paddington Station. Hob telephoned and Annabelle answered. He knew her hesitant, slightly breathy voice.

"Oh, Hob, I'm so glad to hear from you! Where are you calling from?"

"I'm in London."

"That's wonderful! I didn't dare say it in my note, but I was hoping you'd come."

"Well, I'm here. What is all this about? Why did you come to London?"

"Hob, I've got a lot to explain to you, but let's wait until we can meet. Are you free now?"

"Yes."

"Good! Have you got a place we can meet?"

"Do you know Lorne's place?"

"I've been there but I don't remember the address. Would you give it to me again?"

Hob did as told.

"Okay, look, I've got just one thing I have to do. I'll meet you there in an hour."

Hob agreed and hung up. He figured he had time for a quick bite at Lo Tsu Hung's in Queensway. His lacquered duck with lichees was worth the trip to London all by itself.

\* \* \*

He walked back to Lorne's flat. At night, Westbourne Grove looked especially sinister. Dark shapes lurked in doorways, tapping on what might have been bongos. Above London the sky was orange, glaring onto a white sheet. In the diseased elm trees the starlings, those ubiquitious birds of London, rustled their wings, restless and alert, sinister in their patience. An old blind man tapped down the street, his white cane with its one red stripe glistening in the mounting fog. After this it was very welcome for Hob to hear the sound of Lorne's saxophone cutting through the fog that, despite the Clean Air Act, came down like draperies of night over the bleak sidewalks, sifting at last into the sewers, where unclean things floated among the chestnut husks and the soggy red-cross buns left behind by careless schoolboys. He mounted the front steps quickly, let himself in with a key, climbed four flights, let himself in with another key.

When Hob got to Lorne's, he found the lights on and Lorne playing the saxophone in the living room. Two men were there, and they were listening attentively. They were not unusual looking men, just men in perhaps their thirties, one wearing a light raincoat, the other a dark one. The raincoats were open. They both wore dark suits. They had hats, too; one of them had his hat on the couch beside him, the other, sitting in a sagging armchair, had his hat perched on his knee. They were clean-shaven, nice-looking young men.

"Good evening, sir," the one with the light raincoat said. "You would be Mr. Draconian?"

Hob allowed as that's who he was.

"We are Ames and Filbin from the Special Branch. Mr. George Wheaton rang us up. Seems you might need a spot of help. Looking for Mr. Nigel Wheaton, weren't you?"

"Yes, I was. But surely that doesn't involve the Special Branch?"

"We're just doing a favor for Mr. Wheaton. He does some work for us time and again, and we try to reciprocate. He told us you were looking for Mr. Nigel. We are here to take you to him."

"He isn't in any trouble, is he?"

"No, sir. Mr. Nigel was doing a spot of work for us. He expected to be back in touch by the end of the week, but as you told Mr. George it was a matter of some importance, he is prepared to see you now."

"Good, fine," Hob said. He could hardly hear the man in the light raincoat since Lorne's saxophone was wailing at considerable volume. That wasn't like Lorne, who was usually more considerate. "When will he be around?"

"There's a slight problem there," light raincoat said. "Mr. Nigel still has a few more matters to clear up. He'll explain when he sees you. But he asked if you could come with us. We'll take you to him."

"Now? You mean right now?"

"Yes, sir. Mr. Nigel explained it was a matter of some urgency that he see you at once. Something has come up, sir. We are not privy to that information. However, we have the car downstairs and stand ready to take you to him immediately."

Hob nodded, making out the words over the wail of the saxophone. Lorne was really belting it out. Funny. Lorne usually played nothing but calypso and reggae. But this that he was doing seemed to be some sort of old blues tune. The title of it just escaped Hob, though.

Both men were standing now. Dark raincoat was teetering on his heels, stroking his little mustache. Light raincoat was setting his tie straight. Lorne was playing like kingdom come. And then Hob remembered the song. Was it Fats Waller? Louis Armstrong? Then suddenly he had it. That old favorite, "Get out of Town before It's Too Late."

He looked at Lorne, Lorne's eyes were rolling as he took the song up another octave, punching out the melody march style. He looked at the two men, their faces were wooden, expressionless. Light raincoat said, "Shall we be going?" and put a hand lightly on Hob's elbow.

Alarm bells jangled in Hob's brain. He felt sweat springing out on his forehead. "I'll just get my jacket," he said and started for the door.

"I'll come along and keep you company," light raincoat said.

"Fine," said Hob, leaving the room.

The inner staircase was close to the front door. Hob went toward it, light raincoat close behind him. Hob stopped abruptly, and light raincoat almost bumped into him, then took a step backward. Hob lunged for the front door, turning and pulling simultaneously. It was a well-thought-out move, and it deserved to be successful. But he had forgotten that the spring lock was on. The doorknob turned uselessly in his hand. He heard a sound like a grunt of annoyance, fumbled with the lock, and then something hard exploded against the back of his head.

# 7

THERE IS NO beginning and no ending: consciousness is the bad dream to which we awaken from time to time out of the beauty and clarity of the dreamtime, or that which underlies it, the great, all-encompassing Nothing At All. Hob remembered this as he returned to consciousness. His mind was still very far away from what had just taken place. It seemed to him he had been dreaming, and it had something to do with a clearing in a forest, and there had been a girl in a white dress, and some sort of animal had been there, too, small and gray—a badger, though Hob could not remember ever having seen one. The vision or whatever it was faded, and he became conscious of a throbbing pain in his head, toward the back, and of a smell, sharp and piercing but somehow familiar. What was it? Kerosene? No, turpentine. He opened his eyes.

He was in a small, cluttered room filled with the odors of paint and turpentine. There was a bare lightbulb overhead, hanging from a black cord with red threads in it. He was lying on a dark-blue canvas cot.

He was having difficulty focusing. After a moment his vision cleared, and he saw that he was in some sort of a storeroom. There were roughly made shelves, and they were loaded with paint cans and bottles of turpentine. In a corner was a stack of two-by-fours, and in another corner were a broom, its straw head worn down to an angle, and a mop.

Hob rolled off the cot and managed, with some difficulty, to get to his feet. He balanced for a moment until he felt his steadiness return. The room was about seven feet square. There was a door at one side. No windows. No other openings. There was no telephone, either, so there was no way he could call for help. He was on his own.

He took a couple of steps back and forth in the room, to make sure his legs were working all right. Yes, he seemed to be all there. He went to the door and tried to turn the knob. The door was locked. Somehow he had expected that. Still, what do you do with a locked door? He shook the doorknob. It made a loud rattling sound. He tried it again. It wobbled but it didn't open. He put his shoulder against the door and pushed. It wasn't a very powerful push but the door creaked in a satisfying manner and rattled on its hinges. Well, that was more like it. At least it wasn't one of those impenetrable doors that you come across in mysteries of a more esoteric sort. He balanced himself on one leg and planted a kick in the middle of the door. The door shook and groaned. He was about to take another kick at it—this one a really good one that he bet would have split the plywood paneling right down the middle—when a voice from the other side of the door called out, "Here now, take it easy! Don't take my door down!" And then there was the rattle of a key in the lock. Then the key turned, the doorknob turned, and the door opened. There, rocking slightly on his heels and and looking in at him, was a short, pear-shaped man wearing an embroidered waistcoat, in shirtsleeves, with gray worsted pants with knife-sharp creases, his oily black hair immaculately in place, smoking a little cigar, possibly a Willem II— Hob thought he caught the unmistakable spicy tang of Dutch tobacco. On the first finger of his right hand a large emerald glittered.

"Do I have the pleasure of meeting Señor Arranque?" Hob asked.

"That's right. Finally come around, have you?" Arranque said. "Well, come on out and meet the boys."

Hob advanced cautiously through the door into a sort of rustic living room. It was quite large. There was furniture scattered here and there. Tattered overstuffed couches that looked as if they had been retired from some tarted-up second-rate hotel in the Hebrides kept company with a couple of wingback chairs that had done their best flying some years ago.

The "boys" that Arranque had referred to were sitting on the far side of the room in straight-backed wooden chairs on either side of a card table. They seemed to be playing a double solitaire. One of them looked up briefly and waved a negligent finger. The other continued to study his cards.

It took Hob a moment to place them. Then he had it. These were the two ersatz Special Branch guys he'd found in Lorne's apartment, who'd evidently coshed him and brought him here—wherever here was.

"Come on in and take a seat," Arranque said. His voice, while not effusive, was not unfriendly. "What about a nice cup of tea? And a nice aspirin? You'll feel good as new."

Hob tottered into the room. There was an upholstered chair conveniently close to the storeroom door. He dropped into it. The springs were not the best, but he was grateful to be able to assume the reclinlinear position.

"You look awful," Arranque said. His voice might have been mildly concerned. He turned to the boys. They weren't wearing their raincoats now.

"Hey, what did you do to this guy? Drop a sack of bricks on him?"

Light raincoat said, in an aggrieved tone, "I just coshed him once on the back of the head."

"Damn it, I told you not to get rough with him."

"Well, I had to stop him, didn't I? What would you have said if I'd just let him continue his mad bolt to freedom? Eh?"

"All right," Arranque said. Turning to Hob he said, "Sorry about that. There wasn't supposed to be any rough stuff. If you'd just followed the boys like a normal person, there'd have been no trouble."

Light raincoat said to Hob, "I really hated to do it, guv. I'm no thug. But the way you were going, I had to stop you fast or never see you again. And Joe wouldn't have liked that."

Hob said, "What did you do to Lorne?"

"The jig? Nothing. He's probably still playing his saxophone and shaking in his Clark's desert boots. We're not murderers."

Dark raincoat lifted his head from the cards and gave light raincoat a quizzical look. Light raincoat shrugged and said, "Well, not usually. At least we're not *casual* murderers."

Arranque said, "Okay, boys, thanks a lot. Wait in the anteroom, will you?"

They both stood up, giving Arranque looks. Arranque said, "Don't worry about *him*. He's not going to give me any trouble. Are you, sweetheart?"

Hob, sitting back in the padded chair with the bad springs, had to agree, though he didn't say anything. The bogus Special Branch men left, putting on their light and dark raincoats before they went out. Through the opened front door Hob could see that there *was* a bit of a drizzle.

"Sorry for the trouble," Arranque said, "but it was important that I see you right away."

"You could have called and made an appointment," Hob said. "For that matter, how did you know where to find me?"

"It's my business to know things like that," Arranque said. "You've become a problem to me, Mr. Draconian. Did you know that?"

"I had no idea," Hob said.

"Luckily, there's something I can do about it. But that's later. Right now, there's someone to see you."

Arranque opened the door and said, "Come on in, sweetheart." And in walked Annabelle.

# 8

SHE HAD ON a new outfit, a jumpsuit in a color between orange and red and a bright-colored belt to emphasize her small waist. A black-and-white checked silk scarf was thrown across her shoulder.

"Oh, Hob," she said, in a voice that seemed to imply it was Hob's fault that he was here. Then she turned to Arranque, who was standing in the doorway behind her. "You haven't hurt him, have you?"

"He's fine," Arranque said. "Bright and bushy-tailed as the North Americans say."

"Let me speak to him alone," Annabelle said.

She stepped into the room. Arranque left, closing the door behind him.

Annabelle looked around. "Why, this place is filthy!" She dusted off one of the chairs with a tiny perfumed hanky and sat down gingerly. "I don't want to get runs in my stockings. Oh, Hob, why did you follow me to London?"

Hob was already seated. He said, "It's what you wanted me to do, isn't it?"

"Of course I did. But I was hoping in my heart of hearts you'd see through my plan and stay as far away from here as possible. Oh, Hob, you're so clever. I've always admired your intelligence, did you know that? Why couldn't you see that Arranque was certain to have a hold on me, since he hadn't killed me after he killed Stanley? Why couldn't you see that?"

It was not the first time Hob had tried to find a way to deal with a woman's misplaced self-righteousness. Kate had had that quality, too. She had left Hob and blamed him for it. And now Annabelle was blaming Hob for walking into the trap she had set.

"If I had it all to do over again," Hob said, "I would have seen a lot of other things, and acted quite differently. I'd have seen through you at once, for one thing."

"That's what I was hoping you'd do in the first place," Annabelle said. "I feel bad about this, but it's really not my fault. Hob, I refuse to feel guilty."

"Over what?"

"This situation you've set up by following me to London. It's not my fault if you're going to get killed. You're a big boy. You're supposed to be able to look after yourself."

Hob decided to make believe he hadn't heard what she'd said. Maybe she was just being dramatic.

He said soothingly, "No sense guilt-tripping yourself for luring me to this place."

She took it the wrong way. "Damn you, you're being clever now, aren't you? But you're wrong. You can't blame me for this situation! I had to do it!"

"Why?" Hob asked.

"For one thing, my own life was in danger. But another and more important reason is that I have responsibilities! I'm not like you. You can just run around and please yourself. But I have a child in school in Switzerland. A minor child not yet fifteen years old! And no husband! There's no one to take care of her except me. I have to keep myself alive for her."

"I suppose," Hob said, "where a child's welfare is at stake, anything is justified."

"You're being sarcastic, aren't you? Oh, you're such a male chauvinist pig," Annabelle said.

Hob didn't see how that followed, but he didn't respond.

"A real mother would do anything for her kid," Annabelle said.

"That's very moving, Annabelle," Hob said. "Your passion for your child does you great credit. You're a mother and that of course excuses everything. Now, if you're finished scolding me, would you mind telling me what in hell is going on?"

Instead she looked at him, her eyes brimming with tears. "Oh, Hob. You were warned off this thing. Why didn't you give it up?"

Hob said, "I'm a private detective. I was hired to find Stanley's murderer."

"Everybody knows your private detecting is a joke. Why did you push it so far?"

"A joke? What do you mean, a joke?"

"It's something you do to keep up your self-respect. Like half the people on Ibiza say they paint or write or compose. But they're not serious. It's just something to talk about at parties. I thought it was that way with you, too. I had no idea you'd go on trying to find out who killed Stanley."

"He was your friend," Hob pointed out. "I'd think you'd be interested."

She shook her head impatiently. "I know who killed him. And why."

"Would you mind telling me?"

"Stanley was trying to sell the soma I gave him. This was before I knew how stupid a move I'd made. Before I even knew about Arranque and the others. All I knew was Etienne had scored, and he wasn't sharing it with me."

"So the soma came from Etienne?"

"Of course. I thought you knew that."

"I guess I could have figured it out if I'd put my mind to it. And where did Etienne get it?"

"He got it at the meeting in Havana. It was his allotment."

"What meeting in Havana? What allotment?"

She tried to make herself comfortable on the sagging chair. Her skirt was riding up over her beautiful knees. She tugged it down but it rode up again. She forgot about it.

"This was a couple of months ago. Etienne and I were an item for a while, you know. He's a beautiful guy, and really classy. And it seemed like he had all the money in the world. I thought he was rich. He acted like he was rich. I didn't know then that he was on an allowance from his father. It wasn't much. But it came with an airline pass good for going anywhere in the world. He could take me or anyone else he pleased on that pass. And he knew people all over the world. We could stay with his rich friends in all sorts of places, get by without money at all. That's how we got to Havana. Etienne had heard something was going on there. He wanted to check it out."

Annabelle opened her bag and searched until she found a crushed and almost empty pack of cigarettes. She extracted a bent one, straightened it out, and lit it with what looked to Hob like a solid gold Dunhill lighter.

"Well, it turned out this meeting in Havana was a sort of underworld get-together for the purpose of giving out territories."

"Territories?" Hob said.

"In a new dope trade. This soma. It's the latest thing, you know. Etienne had heard about the meeting from some of the men who work for his father. That's Silverio Vargas. He's got a fabulous finca on the island, and he's very rich. But he keeps Etienne on a tight leash. So Etienne decided to go into business for himself."

She paused and inhaled dramatically. "I wasn't paying much attention to all this. Havana was just another resort to me. I spent most of my time on Veradero Beach. Etienne got his consignment or whatever you want to call it, and we went back to Ibiza."

"And back in Ibiza you took his dope?" Hob asked.

"Well, I needed money. Badly. I told you, I've got a kid in a private school in Switzerland. Whatever else I do, I keep the school bills paid so she can stay there. She's going to have a better life than her mom ever had, I can tell you that. And Etienne had understood this from the beginning. He knew that I didn't come free. I couldn't afford that, not with a kid in private school. He understood I had to have money. Not a lot of money, but enough money to pay my bills and take care of my kid. And he said, don't worry, no sweat, I'll get it for you. Only he didn't. And we came back from Havana and all that talk and he had the stuff, the soma, with him, but he didn't have a damned cent in cash money. And my bills were overdue. So finally I had to act. Etienne took his Montessa and went across the island for somebody's birthday. He was gone for two days. While he was away, I took his stash and made a deal with Stanley."

"Why Stanley?" Hob asked.

"I don't know if you ever really knew Stanley. He was good people. He was trustworthy. He said he knew plenty of people in Paris who were interested in a new turn-on. He'd sell the stuff and we'd split what he got fifty-fifty. This wasn't the first deal we'd done. I knew I could trust Stanley.

"Well, Etienne came back, and he was furious when he found his dope missing. I thought I could just wait till he got over it—this wasn't the first time I'd snitched somebody's stash; they always come around after a while. But this time it wasn't that simple. There was all this stuff about soma being a new drug, and people being assigned exclusive territories, and everybody under a vow not to sell any until it was time for everyone to start selling."

"When was the selling supposed to start?" Hob asked.

"After the hotel opening," Annabelle said. "Well, he was mad as hell, Etienne, and he was scared, too, but there wasn't anything I could do about it. Stanley was in Paris, and I didn't even have a telephone number for him. Etienne said we were finished, and he moved out of my place. And he told what happened to Arranque. He had to, I guess. And Arranque came to see me."

"When was this?" Hob asked.

"Just three days after we got back from Havana. It wasn't a very nice meeting. I thought at first I could bluff Arranque, but he beat me up. He was careful not to mark up my face, though. He had a thing for me as soon as he saw me, but he had to do what he had to do. He hurt me, Hob, and I told him everything I knew about Stanley and who he knew in Paris. And the funny thing was, I didn't resent what he did, even though it hurt like hell. I knew he was right, by his standards. He was in charge of all the soma arrangements, and here I was screwing up his deal. He was accountable to people, and I was accountable to him. It's funny how a thing like that can get you close to a person. After he beat me, he was crying—actually crying, Hob—and it came out that he thought I was so beautiful that it broke his heart having to beat me. And he took such great care not to mark me where it'd show. And one thing led to another, and we made love after that, and it was beautiful. And then he told me to keep my mouth shut until he came back, and he left, and the next thing I heard was that he and Etienne had gone to Paris to get hold of Stanley and get the dope back. And then I heard Stanley was dead, so I guess he'd sold the stuff already, and Arranque was doing the best he could to plug the leak."

Hob felt numb at the end of Annabelle's story and didn't know what to say. Finally he said, "Why are you telling me all this?"

"I've got to talk to someone, don't I? And I feel bad about this, Hob. I feel terrible about the spot you're in."

"So what happens now?"

"That's not up to me, Hob. That's up to Ernesto."

"Annabelle, you could get word to someone, couldn't you?"

"Hob, you don't understand. You had your chance. You saw how dangerous it was. You could have walked away and nobody would have bothered you. But you didn't take it. And now you'll just have to take what comes."

"And what about you, Annabelle?"

"I've got my own life to worry about. And believe me, I'm worrying about it plenty. More than you've ever worried about your own."

"Is that your idea of a life? Being a gangster's girlfriend?"

"I'm after a lot more than that, Hob. I've got a chance now at something really big. I'm not going to tell you what it is. I thought you were a friend, but you're really quite unsympathetic. And I'm not going to let you or anything else stand in my way. I've been kicked around enough. It's going to stop now."

"Shit," Hob said.

"Oh! You are no gentleman!" Annabelle cried, and rushed out of the room. The effect was spoiled when she found the door locked and had to knock several times before Arranque let her out.

# 9

"**She's something, isn't** she?" Arranque said, coming into the room and casting an admiring glance back at where Annabelle had been.

"No doubt about it," Hob said.

"I want you to know something," Arranque said. "I want you to know that even though I'm going to have to kill you, it's nothing personal."

"Glad you told me that," Hob said. "It makes it a lot easier."

"Well, I'm hoping it will."

"Maybe I can make it easier on you still."

"How?" Arranque said. "You plan to kill yourself?"

"No. I hope to spare you the necessity of killing me."

"How do you figure to do that?"

"By giving you my word that if you let me out of here, I'll drop this case. Annabelle was right. It's too rich for my blood."

"You're not serious, are you?" Arranque asked.

"Perfectly serious."

"I wish I could believe you," Arranque said. "But I don't. I'm afraid I'm going to have to fix your clock."

"Beg pardon?"

" 'Fix your clock' is a North American expression for 'kill you.' "

"Oh. I've been out of the country for a while."

"Try to put yourself in my shoes. Even if I believed you, I still couldn't let you live. I have to make an example of you. I have to show what happens to people when they fool around with soma people. This isn't no tiny little operation. This is the big time. We need to establish respect from the start. Like the mafia's got respect. You know what I mean?"

Hob nodded. He saw no reason to be difficult just now.

"I have to do something dramatic with you," Arranque said. "Something that'll get people's attention. Something spectacular. Or at least interesting."

"What did you have in mind?" Hob asked.

"I've got a couple ideas," Arranque said. "But it would be premature to talk about them now. Try to take it easy, seamus. I'll get back to you soon."

Hob decided it was not the time to tell Arranque the word was "shamus" rather than "seamus." No sense getting the guy riled up at you.

And that was the last Hob heard until almost an hour later.

"All right," Arranque said. "Tie him up and bring him out."

The two bogus Special Branch men bound Hob's hands behind him with a length of transparent plastic cord. Then he did the same for Hob's feet. Then the other man took out a cigarette lighter and applied it to the knots, warming them but not setting them on fire. The knots melted into blobby masses the size of crab apples.

"Nobody unties those knots," one of them said. The other nodded.

"Okay, carry him out here."

The two men lugged Hob out of the room, and, following Arranque, down a short flight of stairs to the main floor of the factory room. Here, beneath overhead fluorescents hanging from chains, the skeletons and corpses of once busy machines littered the floor. The place seemed very old. Hob guessed that most of the equipment dated from the early years of the twentieth century. Not that he was any expert.

"Put him on the chute," Arranque said.

The chute was waist high, an open-sided metal slide about three feet wide with sides about two feet high. It extended at an angle from a point in the factory wall near the ceiling and extended across the room at a slope to where it entered a bulky metal object the size of a garage, whose function Hob could not guess, though he feared the worst.

The bogus Special Branch men laid Hob on the chute on his back. Hob found that he was lying on rollers. Arranque walked to a wall and did something Hob couldn't see. Machine noises started up. They came from belts beneath the chute, and from the garage-sized object ahead of Hob's feet and about fifteen yards away.

"This gadget is an ore crusher," Arranque said to Hob. "The chunks of ore are carried on this conveyor belt and fed into the crushing machine. It's straight ahead of you. If you crane your neck a little, you can see it."

Hob craned his neck and saw that a panel had slid open on the garage-sized machine, revealing two long steel rollers. The rollers had begun to turn—slowly, ponderously at first, then with increased speed. It didn't take a genius to figure out that anything coming down the conveyor belt would be brought in between the two rollers and crushed to something small and, in his case, bloody.

Annabelle appeared and walked over to Hob.

"Hob," she said, "I'm really sorry about this. But it's not my fault. I did warn you."

Hob couldn't quite bring himself to believe that all this was happening. He said, "Stop apologizing and get me out of here."

"Oh, Hob," she said, and began to cry.

"I'm not really a cruel guy," Arranque said. "But I need to make an impression on my partners. Especially the Indians. When they hear of this, they'll know I'm someone to be reckoned with."

From where he was lying, Hob couldn't think of anything amusing to say. He heard another click. Arranque had turned another switch. The roller wheels under Hob began to move very slowly.

"Let's get out of here," Arranque said to Annabelle, adding, "and stop that sniveling, will you?"

"I just hate to see this happening to someone from Ibiza," Annabelle said, drying her eyes with a tiny handkerchief.

"He was warned," Arranque said, as if that explained everything. "Take it easy, Mr. Draconian. I'm off to Ibiza now. Your buddy Nigel ought to be just about finished hanging my pictures. When he's done, I'll send him to hell to join you."

Hob heard more footsteps, receding. And then there was nothing but him riding a conveyor belt into the mouth of hell. To put it one way.

# 10

WHEN HE WAS alone, Hob's first thought was a curiously optimistic one. There was little doubt in his mind that Arranque was some sort of a loser.

Proof of this was the fact that Hob's demise hadn't been planned out with meticulous care. Apparently there had been no time to hold a rehearsal. By wiggling around and wedging his body sideways in the chute, and pressing with his head and feet, Hob was able to stop himself from being carried down to the crushing cylinders. He held himself in this position and tried to think of what to do next. It was difficult to concentrate in all that noise. He couldn't hear anything above the grinding of gears and the roar of the motor impelling the contraption, but he let enough time pass for Arranque and the others to have gotten into their car and driven away. Then it was time to get himself out of this.

Harry Houdini, with his incredible contortionist talents, would have had little difficulty getting off of the conveyor belt. But Hob was no Houdini. He tried to get his bound feet above the side of the belt but couldn't find enough leverage to do that, and the conveyor belt carried him another five feet toward the grinding cylinders before he gave it up and wedged himself again. His motion toward the cylinders stopped. But he couldn't do anything about getting himself off the conveyor belt while he was wedging himself that way.

At least he was safe for the moment. It took some effort to keep himself from sliding down toward the slowly revolving cylinders.

It gave him the most precious boon of all: time to think, to plan, to come up with the brilliancy that would get him out of this mess.

Unfortunately, no useful thoughts came. He breathed the sooty air of the factory, listened to the clanking of the gears as the conveyor belt rotated slowly beneath him. It was curiously difficult to concentrate. Images flitted across his mind, vague and indistinct, black-and-white snapshots of Ibiza, grayed-out prints of a Paris he might never see again. He was in a curious state: tense and pumped up, but with a great fatigue working in him. His back and leg muscles were trembling from the effort of keeping himself pressed against the sides of the conveyor belt.

Minutes passed. No loss, no gain, but he was getting tired.

A sense of hopelessness started to seep into his mind. Yes, he had found a momentary way of arresting his death. But it required a constant effort, and he was starting to wear out. He didn't begrudge making the effort, but how long could he keep it up? How long would he need to keep it up? As far as he knew, nobody knew where he was. Could he expect somebody to come by? A watchman, an area guard? A tourist, or a kid exploring the place? No, there was no reason he could think of for anyone to come by and interrupt his slow slide toward death.

Even as he was thinking this, he felt himself carried a few feet along the conveyor belt. His burdened leg muscles had relaxed of their own accord. He checked his motion at once, pushing hard, feeling the rollers turn under his back. He had about twenty-five feet to go before he was pulled into what he had come to think of as the jaws of death.

Time to take stock, figure something out. There had to be something he could do. He strained against his bonds. There was no give. He couldn't see the knots, but he knew they had been melted into roughly spherical blobs. There were no loose ends to work with, and the knots he could reach were sealed tight.

Lying there on the bed of the conveyor belt, Hob couldn't see much, only his tied feet and the shiny metal sides of the conveyor. He levered himself up to a partial sitting position, giving ground on the conveyor belt so he could look into his possibilities. He lay back again, bracing and arresting his progress. He had noticed only one thing that might be of use: The top side of the chute, the left side as he looked down it, was not smooth metal. Something must have fallen against it. The metal rim ten feet ahead of him was bent and torn. If he could get his bound hands over the side and then let himself be carried forward, there was a possibility the jagged metal would sever the plastic with which he was bound.

The only difficulty was, if it didn't work, if the plastic cord didn't sever, he'd be carried right on into the rollers.

How tough was that plastic cord?

Could he just lie there, wedged in, and think it over for a while?

Not for long. His tensed muscles kept releasing on him, easing up, losing him a few inches here, a foot or so there. Waiting was a losing game.

All right. There was nothing to do but go for it.

Hob released his muscles, felt himself carried along the moving belt toward the rotating cylinders, tried to get his bound hands over the edge of the belt, failed by several inches, fell back, felt himself carried along, brought up his bound feet with a wrenching motion, arched his back and thrust again, this time getting his ankles onto the upper rim of the belt. Now he tried to bring pressure to his ankles by arching his back, feeling the rough metal tear at the plastic cord; hearing the growl of the rotating cylinders; feeling the plastic slip and tear, slip and tear; realizing the plastic wasn't going to part in time; bending at the waist and seeing the cylinders approaching his feet; pulling his legs in and wedging against the sides again. He was about three feet from the rotating cylinders. His body was quivering with muscle fatigue.

And at that terrible moment, he heard the most welcome sound of all: George Wheaton's voice coming from somewhere above him and to his left, calling out, "I say, Hob! Hang on, old boy!"

And then a most unwelcome sound after that: George's voice saying, "Have you any idea how to turn this damned thing off?"

George, panting, out of breath, one trouser ripped from slipping on a pile of rubble outside, was looking at a crudely constructed switchboard set onto the wall of the observation booth above the factory floor. There were some twenty small switches on that board, a dozen buttons, and two big knife switches. Nothing was written under or above any of the instruments. George hesitated for a moment, then pulled one of the big knife switches. Nothing discernable happened. He tried the other one. Another dud.

"Confound it!" George muttered, and pressed the leftmost button. The motor of an overhead crane whirred into life. George pursed his lips and pushed another switch. The lights in the factory went off, though the machinery continued to run unabated. George punched wildly at the buttons and managed to get the lights on again. "Hang on!" George cried.

"Aieeeee!" Hob cried as he felt his treacherous muscles let go again and found himself carried to the revolving rollers.

And there he made a discovery.

His feet, though not unusually large, were too big to fit into the two-inch aperture between the rollers. He pushed and kicked against the revolving cylinders with his bound feet. The rollers turned and bumped under him. But there was no way he could be pulled between the cylinders.

Unless it caught his pants leg. Or picked up a shoelace.

No problem with his pants legs. His efforts had hiked them halfway to his knees. But looking down his body, he saw that his left shoelace was untied, the ends flapping free, dancing up and down the cylinders, just missing being caught and pulled in.

"George!" Hob screamed. "Forget about turning it off! Just pull me out of here!"

"I'm coming!" George shouted back, and raced down the stairs to the factory floor.

Hob kept on kicking at the cylinders, his neck craned to watch the flying shoelace of his left sneaker dancing in the air, kicking, kicking, trying to keep it free.

And then the shoelace floated through the air with an almost palpable malevolence, and dropped in between the cylinders.

At that same moment, George had his arms around him and was trying to lift him out of the conveyer-belt bed.

The cylinder took up the shoelace's slack and began tugging at Hob's foot.

For a few moments it was a tug of war between George and the cylinders, with Hob's shoelace as the rope.

Hob remembered at that moment that his shoelace was woven rather than a single strand. He had thought it looked nice.

The damned thing wouldn't part.

The cylinders were pulling him in foot first.

And then Hob's sneaker came off and was pulled between the cylinders, and with one final wrench George had him off the conveyer belt, and both men were sprawled on the factory's grimy floor.

# 11

BACK AT GEORGE'S house, George found a change of clothing for Hob.

"Just old gardening togs," George said. "But they'll have to do until we can find something better. And I think my Clark's will fit you."

"May I use your phone?" Hob said.

He tried to call Jean-Claude again in Paris. By some miracle, he got him on the first try.

Hob asked, "What's happening? Where have you been?"

"I thought Nigel has explained it all to you by now."

"That's what I'm calling about. Where is Nigel? What's been happening?"

"Ah," Jean-Claude said, "then you don't know about the letter."

"I know about the letter but not what was in it. Damn it, Jean-Claude, talk!"

Jean-Claude told Hob that soon after Hob had left for Ibiza, a telegram arrived for him. Telegrams always have an air of urgency about them, so Nigel had opened it. As far as Jean-Claude could remember, it was from Santos and had been sent from his island nation of San Isidro. It had complimented Hob on his fine work in the recent case involving Aurora and Max. Santos had been on the other side then, but he had not been personally affected when Hob solved the case. He had been paid for his participation up front, and so was able to watch the events with a certain philosophical attitude that was entirely native to his personality. In any event, the telegram wasn't about that case. Santos appreciated the fine work Hob and his agency had done. He had a little matter of his own that had recently come up. He didn't want to discuss it in a telegram or letter, or even on the telephone. But he said that if Hob or one of his men would care to come to San Isidro, he could show him the hospitality of the island and discuss the job with them. If Hob didn't want it, at least he could enjoy a few days in the sunny Caribbean. He had instructed Cooks Travel in Paris to have an open return ticket to San Isidro prepared and looked forward to Hob's arrival.

"That's great," Hob said. "Why didn't anyone tell me about this?"

"We tried," Jean-Claude said. "But you were off in Ibiza trying to find the killer of Stanley Bower. We tried to telephone you at Sandy's bar, but evidently you never got our message. So Nigel and I discussed it and finally decided that he would go on behalf of the agency and check it out."

"So Nigel went to San Isidro," Hob said. "What happened when he arrived?"

"I wish I could tell you," Jean-Claude said.

But Hob thought he knew; it must have been Santos who set up the deal with Arranque.

George made him a nice cup of tea. The way George explained it, his division, the Future Developments group, had had its eye on the development of soma almost from the start. It was one of the big ones, one of the things that could change the future. But George's brief was observational only. He was specifically forbidden by law to interfere in any way. After the many disasters of British intelligence, this was the only way a long-range prediction group was allowed to operate.

"I took the liberty of doing something when I saw how things were going," George said. "I did it for Nigel even more than for you. I had you followed. When I learned where you were, I came after you myself."

"Many thanks," Hob said.

"Officially, nothing happened at all. We're not supposed to interfere. Only observe."

"What am I supposed to do now?" Hob asked.

"The best thing will be for you to get back to Ibiza," George said. "I'm counting on you to get Nigel out of this."

"Nigel's on Ibiza now?"

"Correct. He's doing the final supervision of the hanging of the pictures for the big hotel opening tomorrow. I want him out of it, Hob. I've telephoned and can't get through to him. I can't go through official channels. The Spanish police don't want to hear about this. But you can tell him. You can do it."

Hob nodded, though he wasn't really in the mood for getting into this thing again.

"I'll run you to the airport myself," George said.

"Good for you," Hob said. George's manner was contagious.

# FOUR

# IBIZA

# 1

HOB WASHED UP in the small toilet on his Iberia flight from London to Ibiza. A stewardess even found him a razor, but no shaving cream. He made do with a tiny bar of soap. There was nothing he could do about George's old gardening togs, however. They would look out of place anywhere but in George's garden. He resolved to change them at the first opportunity.

The plane landed at Ibiza at just past 1 P.M. Standard Hippie Time: a little too late for what he had planned. He wanted to get to the party for the hotel opening, but he had no invitation. Something told him this was one gate he wouldn't be able to crash. His only hope was Big Bertha, who he knew had an invitation—and a habit of being late for everything.

A taxi took him from the airport into Ibiza City, snarled its way through the dense summer traffic, negotiated the turns up into the Dalt Villa, and finally left him off a block below Bertha's flat. Hob hurried to her door and slammed the big iron knocker. No answer. He slammed the knocker a few times more, and, still getting no response, walked out into the street and shouted up to her open windows.

"Bertha! Are you there? It's Hob."

After the fifth repetition of this, a tousle-haired adolescent poked his head out of the small restaurant next door and said, "It doesn't matter if you're Hob or not. She's not there."

"How do you know?"

"Because I saw her drive away. You just missed her."

*"Carrai!"* Hob said. It was the customary Ibicenco response for anything that goes wrong through no fault of one's own.

"You musta seen her car as you came up," the youth said. "It's that mustard-yellow Simca. Couldn't miss it."

Now that he mentioned it, Hob did remember such a car. He had been so fixated on mentally urging the taxi around the hairpins to Bertha's that he hadn't noticed Bertha passing.

"Hell and damnation!" Hob said. He looked at the kid and after a moment recognized him. It was Ralphie, Sandra Olson's second son. He looked about fourteen. There was supposed to be something peculiar about him: Either he was actually twelve and looked old for his age or he was actually seventeen and looked young for his age. Hob couldn't remember which.

"What are you doing here, Ralphie?" Hob asked.

"I work in the kitchen. It's a summer job, until school starts again."

"I really need to get hold of Bertha," Hob said.

"You got a car? She doesn't drive very fast. You might catch up to her if you know where she's going."

Hob shook his head. "No car. I'll have to go back down to the Pena and find a taxi."

"Where's she going?"

"The new hotel opening in San Mateo."

"If you had a dirt bike," Ralphie said, "you could catch her before she got there."

"A what?"

"You know, a scrambler. An off-road motorcycle. Once you're out of the city, you could take a shortcut over the hills."

"I don't have a dirt bike."

"I do. And I'm for hire."

"What about your job here?"

"Pablo will cover for me. A thousand pesetas. Is it a deal?"

"You're on," Hob said.

Ralphie went back inside the restaurant. There was a gabble of high-speed Ibicenco. Then Ralphie came out again wheeling a fire-red Bultaco Matador 250cc motorcycle with knobby wheels and high fenders. He kicked it into life. The machine's roar, there in the narrow street, echoing off the close-packed buildings, was deafening.

"Climb aboard," Ralphie said.

Hob had a moment to doubt the wisdom of riding with a high-school kid or perhaps younger who knew he was in a hurry. Still, what else was there to do? He got on—and grabbed Ralphie in time to prevent falling over backward as the boy gunned the machine.

They sped down the slick, steeply tilted, cobblestoned streets of the upper city, cutting through a back lane on their way, taking corners heeled over like a sailboat in a gale. The motorcycle had no horn, but pedestrians scattered at the high-pitched bellow of its motor. Twice Hob's feet were jarred off the back pegs, and he had to struggle to stay aboard. The square-vented exhaust housing was close to his thigh, and he had to stay on without frying. They finally got through town without killing themselves or anyone else, even managing to avoid an Ibicenco hound sunning itself on the sidewalk they had to cut across to avoid oncoming cars as they plunged peremptorily onto the main road.

It was a little better after that. At least it was level. Ralphie twisted the throttle to its stop and held it there, and the motorcycle howled up the two-lane road. But the Bultaco wasn't a road bike and couldn't do much better than 80 miles an hour or so, so it wasn't quite as dangerous as it sounded.

"Neat, huh?" Ralphie screamed over his shoulder.

"Keep your eyes on the road!" Hob screamed back.

They drove at full bore for about fifteen minutes, until they came to where the road divided, the right fork going to Santa Eulalia, the left to Santa Gertrudis, San Mateo, and San Juan. Ralphie took the left fork. Just a few minutes up the road he slowed and turned onto a dirt road that led across the hills instead of winding around as the main road did. It was a pretty good road, and if you ignored the possible danger of meeting horse-driven carts around blind curves, as Ralphie did, you could make pretty good time. The road leveled out on top of the hill, and they turned off again, speeding through a sparse pine forest and dodging the odd boulder that nature had set down for the purpose of providing a slalom course for aspiring motocross drivers. Then Ralphie braked hard, bringing the bike to a stop on a hilltop. He pointed to his left and down. A few hundred feet below, Hob could the see hotel's private road, with Bertha's mustard-yellow Simca—or one just like it—stopped at a little one room cementblock house that stood just beside an entrance cut through a high masonry wall. Hob could see the uniformed guard at the gate checking something, Bertha's invitation no doubt, and then waving her through.

"Well, we almost made it," Ralphie said. "I coulda brought us down this hill in about two minutes. Wanna try anyway?"

Hob looked at the hill, which was pitched at an angle that looked impossible even for a downhill skier, and thanked his lucky stars they hadn't arrived five minutes earlier.

"What I want you to do now," Hob said, "is take me, slowly, to where the hotel road joins the San Mateo road. I'm too late to catch Bertha, but somebody I know is sure to come along."

Ralphie drove back over the hills to the main road, and then down it to where the hotel road crossed. He seemed sorry that the adventure was over. But the thousand peseta note that Hob gave him, and the extra five hundred he threw in for good luck, cheered him considerably. Ralphie took off in a cloud of dust and a sparkling of gravel; Hob found a rock by the side of the road and sat down to wait.

It took a little time to regain his equilibrium after that ride. But after his heart rate had returned to normal, he was able to enjoy the day—a perfect Ibiza summer afternoon, warm but not sultry, with a light breeze blowing and the salt tang of the ocean not far away.

A taxi passed, filled with people Hob didn't know. He dug around in his pockets, found a crumbled pack of Ducados that he had transferred from his clothes in London, found a book of matches with three matches left, lighted up, and relaxed in the sun. It was peaceful there, and Hob had had a difficult night. He decided to close his eyes for just a moment. . . .

"Hey, Hob!"

Hob woke up with a start. He was surprised at himself, drifting off like that. But the warm comforting glow of Ibiza sunshine, the lisp of leaves in the nearby trees, and not even a ripple of rain, had lulled him to sleep in spite of himself. Now, looking up, he saw a battered Citröen station wagon stopped in the road alongside him. Peering out from the driver's seat was the good-natured face of his friend Juanito, owner and cook of Juanito's Restaurant in Santa Eulalia.

"Hello, Juanito," Hob said. "What are you doing out here?"

"I'm catering the appetizers for the hotel party," Juanito said. "This is the second load the boys and I are bringing in."

There were two waiters from Juanito's restaurant in the backseat of the station wagon. Hob knew them by sight. They exchanged nods.

"And what about you?" Juanito said.

"I'm working on a case," Hob said.

Juanito's eyes grew round, and he nodded slowly. For any of the permanent foreign community to do anything resembling work was notable.

"Does your case bring you to the hotel?" Juanito asked. "Not that I'm trying to be nosy . . ."

"No problem, Juanito," Hob said. "I'm on a case which requires me to attend the new hotel party. Unfortunately I don't have an invitation, and I missed Bertha, who was going to take me in."

"You'll need an invitation to get in all right," Juanito said. "They're pretty careful at the gate. If I could be of any help . . ."

"You could do one of two favors for me," Hob said. "When you're inside, you could find Bertha and tell her I'm out here on the road. Maybe she could come out again and get me in."

"That's easy enough," Juanito said. "What's the other?"

"I scarcely dare suggest this," Hob said, "but if you could see your way clear to bringing me in as a waiter . . ."

Juanito nodded. "It's an important case, Hob?"

"Very important."

"Then I'll take you in myself. You haven't got proper clothes, however." He looked at Hob, eyes narrowed, taking in George's gardening togs, which seemed far more eccentric in Ibiza than in England. Then he turned to one of the waiters in the back. "Enrique, you're about Hob's size. Would you mind changing clothes with him and missing the party?"

"What about my overtime pay?"

"I'm sure Hob will reimburse you."

"I'll do better than that. I'll double whatever you were going to get. And as for you, Juanito—"

Juanito waved a hand. "Don't even consider paying me. This is the most exciting thing I've had happen since I left Salt Lake City."

The exchange of clothes was made behind a convenient bush. Enrique's waiter's outfit fit Hob tolerably well, except for the waist, which was three inches too wide. But Enrique had a cummerbund, which held everything up nicely.

Juanito said, "Enrique, you don't mind walking back into San Mateo? I'll pick you up when I leave."

"A walk will be a pleasure on a day this. You'll find me in Bar La Legión." To Hob he said, "Try not to get blood on my clothes, Mr. Detective."

Hob said he would do his best to avoid that. And then they were on their way to the hotel. The guard didn't even look at Hob or the other waiter. He had already seen Juanito on his first time through, and now he just waved him past.

"We're in," Juanito said. "What now?" He had driven the Citröen around to the kitchen entrance in back.

"I'd appreciate your finding me some light work to do. I need to look around, see if I can find Nigel. You haven't seen him, have you?"

Juanito shook his head. "But I've been in the kitchen just about all the time. Would you like to carry a tray of hors d'ouevres around?"

"That would suit me just fine," Hob said.

Juanito had prepared half a dozen trays of appetizers back in his restaurant. Now he, Hob, and the other waiter, whose name was Paco, carried them into the hotel kitchen. There Juanito set up an assortment on a big serving tray. Hob walked into the main hotel area carrying *pimientos rellenos de merluza, canelónes de legumbres, gambas con huevos rellenos, gambas al ajillo,* and Juanito's specialty, stolen from Chef Gregorio Camarero, *boquerónes rellenos de jamón y espinaca.*

From the outside, the hotel had appeared to be a large multilevel structure, part of it wood, part fieldstone. The main wing was three stories high, with balconies facing the little valley that the hotel also owned. There were tennis courts and a nine-hole golf course, two outdoor swimming pools, a jai alai court, the only one in the Balearics, and a lot of other stuff Hob hadn't had time to notice, including a stable. Inside, in the main hotel lobby, there was soft hotel lighting and a lot of blond wood and oversized leather couches and a lot of people standing around with drinks in their hands and talking the sort of bright, witty chatter for which Ibiza expatriates are justly famous.

So there was Hob, playing at being waiter in a pair of black pants with black satin stripes down the legs and with a waist two or three sizes too large for him and held up with a crimson cummerbund wound five times around his waist, tight enough to keep his pants up, which meant too tight for comfort. And to top it off he also had on a silly little matador-type jacket. He held the big serving tray in both hands—no insoucient balancing on the palm of one hand for him—weaving his slow and awkward way through the densely packed chattering guests in the main ballroom, or whatever they called it.

Looking around, he observed that the male guests were wearing the latest creations from Hombre or Yes! boutiques, while the women had on a variety of layered white garments with flowing ends that were all the rage in Ibiza that year. And Hob was worrying not for the first time that he wasn't carrying a gun or knife or other deadly device because his treatment at Arranque's hands back in London was still clear in his mind. But what the hell; he had prevailed in the past without weapons, and with a little luck he'd do so again. What counted for a lot right now was that he hadn't run into any of his old friends here so far—and more important, he hadn't run into Arranque, who was presumably the host. But of course it couldn't go on like that, not in Ibiza, and so he found himself suddenly proferring his tray of appetizers to someone he knew: Luis Carlos, who owned the Kilometer Zero restaurant on the road to San Lorenzo.

Luis Carlos gaped at him but couldn't quite place him. He was not quite sober, of course. His bewilderment was due to the fact that in Ibiza, context is everything. Luis politely took *huevos duros con atún* on a napkin and moved on, showing no sign of recognition.

Hob spotted Arranque across the room and turned quickly so as not to be recognized.

Hob was feeling curious. It was strange how wearing a waiter's outfit could affect your very mentality, and so now he found something servile and cringing in his manner, and he quickly overcompensated for it by becoming overbearing and insolent. He was in that mood when he finally ran into Big Bertha.

"Hob!" Bertha said. "What are you doing in that outfit?"

"I'm pretending to be a waiter serving appetizers," Hob said. "Quick, pretend to take one."

Bertha picked one off the tray and looked at it curiously. "Is it really an appetizer?"

"It's no more a real appetizer than I'm a real waiter. You only pretend to eat it. Listen, have you seen Nigel?"

She shook her head so vehemently that her large dangle earrings danced and jangled. "Was I supposed to?"

"You are now. If you see him, tell him he's in danger and had better get out of here at once."

She gave him a curious look. It looked as if she was about to ask him why he couldn't tell Nigel himself. But luckily she remembered that she knew nothing about the private detective business, nodded, and moved on.

# 2

NIGEL WAS IN the second-floor gallery, the jewel of Arranque's eye, the place where he planned to show class. The corridor was a hundred and sixty-five feet long by twenty feet wide, illuminated by recessed overhead lighting that was pretty good for showing you where you were walking but not very good for showing off the pictures. Not that there was much to show off. The pictures were not much to look at. But they were indeed genuine oil paintings, framed, and Arranque was proud of himself for having acquired them.

Nigel was not so proud of his part in the acquisition. These paintings, chosen from the odds and ends of Posonby's warehouse stock, framed and lighted like masterpieces, had seemed a funny idea back in England. Now, in Ibiza, where every second person was an art critic and half the foreign community was made up of aspiring painters, it seemed not funny at all. It had suddenly occured to Nigel that *he* would be judged on these works, not Arranque, who couldn't be expected to know any better.

Nigel had three men working with him, Arranque's men detailed to the task. One was on a ladder, trying to hang the painting; another was holding the painting's lower edge; and the third was following up with dust cloth and feather duster. Nigel had set it all up with his usual care, using a ruler and a right angle, making sure that everything was well squared away. His heart sank a little as he looked at the painting he was hanging now. It was a fruity Italian landscape drawn in the worst possible taste, and filled with fountains, hills, cypresses, a shepherd, a shepherdess, and even a fawn, yet.

"A little bit more to the right," Nigel said. At least he could ensure that they were hung straight.

"Look," Nigel said to the third man, "you have to go to a window and beat out the dust cloth. Otherwise you're just transferring dust from one painting to another." The man gave a surly nod and continued exactly as he had been doing.

At this point Arranque entered. He had on some sort of semiformal resort clothing he'd picked up in Miami—a green plaid afternoon jacket, the green too bright, even the black too bright. He had on tricky Italian sandals completely out of style with the Ibiza style of sandal. There was a light lavender dress handkerchief with red piping around the edges in the upper left-hand pocket of the jacket. The line of the jacket was ruined first of all by Arranque's shape—a stocky, potbellied shape on which nothing svelte could be fitted except perhaps a giant potholder—and second, by the slight but noticeable bulge in his righthand pocket that might have been caused by a sack of cookies, though Nigel rather doubted it.

"Ah, Nigel, almost finished, I see."

"Yes, Ernesto. Just two more to go. How do you think it looks?"

"Splendid," Arranque said. "I've been in the Prado, you know, and they have some exhibitions that look no better than this."

That was, of course, the most pathetic artistic judgment of the decade—perhaps even the century—but Nigel hadn't been hired to correct it.

"I think it looks rather good myself," Nigel said, referring to the way the paintings were hung rather than the intrinsic merit of that which was hanging.

"When you're finished, come down to my office. The boys will show the way. I've got a little surprise for you."

"That's nice," Nigel said, thinking: bonus for a job well done.

"And by the way," Arranque said, "a friend of yours is here at the party."

"Oh, indeed?"

"Yes. Señor Draconian has paid us a visit."

"That's nice," Nigel said. "I've been wanting to get in touch with him. Where is he?"

"He's downstairs in the main lobby making himself useful passing out the appetizers. I'm sure he'll be delighted to see you."

Arranque left. Nigel thought to himself, This Arranque fellow has some rough edges, but he's quite a good fellow in his way.

Nigel had never been known as a good judge of character.

**3**

WHEN HOB RETURNED to the kitchen, Juanito was warming up the warm appetizers and chilling down the cold ones.

"Ah, Hob, how's it going?"

"Fine," said Hob.

"If you wouldn't mind," Juanito said, "there's something I'd like you to do. Would you help Pepe get some wine out of the cellar? We want the Château Yquem '69."

"Sure thing," Hob said, "I've been wanting a look down there anyway."

He accepted the key and a flashlight from Juanito and followed Pepe out of the kitchen to a short passageway, through a door, and down a few steps to another door. Hob unlocked it and led the way into the cellar.

The place appeared to be quite old, dug for the finca that had been here before the hotel. A string of bare electric bulbs was strung along the walls. Hob found a pull switch and turned them on. By their dim light he could see that the walls were roughhewn out of limestone, unfinished. The place was cool and dry inside. Nice after the heat of the day outside.

Working his way along, Hob saw that the cellar extended into a natural rock cavern. The cases of wine and champagne were stacked up along the walls. Hob walked past the last case and shone his flashlight into the darkness beyond. The passageway slanted down, and he could see no end to it.

"You guys get started," Hob called to the waiters. "Find the Château Yquem and take some of it up. I'll be right with you."

He continued deeper and deeper into the rock that lay beneath the hotel. After fifty or so feet the cavern began to narrow. It was here that Hob found a pile of boxes covered with a green tarpaulin. It blended so well with the walls that he almost walked past it.

The tarp had been tied into place around the boxes. Hob untied one of the corners and pulled it back. He found a stack of wooden crates. He got out his Swiss Army knife and, with considerable difficulty, levered up one of the boards, almost cutting his finger in the process. At last he got it and saw that inside, packed in excelsior, were a number of small green objects. Lifting one of them, he shone the flashlight beam on it. Yes, it was one of his green bottles all right. It was filled with a heavy, liquid substance. He shook it. The liquid moved slowly, with a sleepy, luxurious motion that Hob could almost describe as evil. He didn't think it was a sample size of Lavoris. This was soma.

Hob replaced the bottle in the excelsior and put the top strip back on. He retied the tarp, leaving it more or less as he had found it. Then he hurried back to the kitchen, bringing the last half-dozen bottles of Château Yquem with him.

After depositing the bottles in the kitchen for Juanito to open, Hob picked up another tray of appetizers and went out again.

He could see that some of the guests were already leaving. It was late afternoon. The real festivities, which were only for the hotel's backers and special guests, would begin in an hour or so. He still hadn't found Nigel. But at last he did spot Bertha.

"Going now?" he asked her.

"In a few minutes. Do you need a ride?"

"I can't leave yet. But I want you to get hold of Ramón at the Guardia Civil barracks in Ibiza. Tell him this is an illegal gathering, and we need the services of him and his men in the patent-leather three-cornered hats."

"Hob, have you been drinking? Doping?"

"No, I'm just high on role-playing. Will you do what I ask? You are working for the agency, aren't you?"

"Of course I am. And frankly, this party is a stone bore anyway. Can I put this canapé back on your tray?"

"Yes, but don't let anyone see you. That's it. Off you go now."

# 4

HOB, STILL KEEPING an eye open for Nigel, wandered around the hotel. He strolled into the Lilac Room and saw Vana, his rescuer from Arranque's hoods of several nights ago.

Vana said, "It is good to see you, senhor. There is someone over here who would like to meet you."

Vana pointed to a very sunburned, balding man sitting in a wing chair in the corner and smoking a cigar.

"Allow me to produce my patron, Senhor Silverio Vargas."

The two men shook hands. Vargas indicated a chair. Vana moved a discreet distance away, close enough to be at hand if anything should come up, far enough so that he was not eavesdropping on the conversation.

Vargas said, "Let's get right to the point. Tell me, Mr. Draconian, what is your interest in this situation with Arranque?"

"A man I know, Stanley Bower, was killed in Paris. His brother hired me to find his murderer.

"And you suspect Senhor Arranque?"

Hob nodded. "You could say that."

Vargas smiled and thought a long time before he spoke. "You are not, by any chance, out to make a name for yourself by breaking a big drug connection?"

"No, I'm not," Hob said. "I've told you my interest in the case. I have another friend who may be involved. Unwittingly. I want to get him clear, too."

"If you could do that much, would you stay clear of the drug connection?"

"I would."

"How can I know that?"

"Hey, look at me," Hob said. "My face is my fortune."

Vargas studied Hob's face for a while. Then smiled again. "It is a good face. Very Norte Americano. Ingenuous. Determined. Idealistic. Naive."

"You've got me down to a T," Hob said.

"And facetious. But never mind that. Mr. Draconian, I think our interests may intersect here. I think we might be able to help each other."

"I'm not going to join your gang, if that's what you're getting at."

"No, no! You really are delightful, Mr. Draconian. But I suppose you get results in your own way. No, let us put some cards on the table. You probably know by now that a very large drug operation is soon to begin."

"I've been under that impression."

"Just between us, I have an interest in it."

"I won't tell a soul."

"Thank you. More to the point, my son, Etienne, is also involved in this matter. He got into it entirely without my knowledge. To the point of danger."

"Tell me about it," Hob said. "If you want to, that is."

"I think that I do. Vana has told me you are someone to confide in. Vana is never wrong. Well, let's have a little drink, and a cigar, and I'll begin."

Vargas got up and poured drinks. He opened a cedar-lined box, and Hob accepted a Havana like they used to make Havanas and still do if you're not an American. They lit up.

"My son's involvement in this matter," Vargas said, "is really my fault. Vana has told me so, and I might as well confess it up front. I kept the boy on too tight a leash. I didn't give him enough money. I thought an unlimited airline ticket good year-round for any place on the earth, and his quite generous allowance, would be sufficient. I wanted him to steady himself, to be something more than a rich man's son." Vargas puffed his cigar into life and regarded the glowing tip for a moment. "I wanted him to be a lawyer, to move in the best society, to enjoy all the advantages that I never had. I came up the hard way, Mr. Draconian, and in a hard world where you had to take what you wanted."

Hob leaned back. One of the perils of the private detective trade was that wealthy men were forever telling you their life stories. In this case, however, it looked as if it might be an interesting story. And the cigar was very fine.

"The fact is," Vargas said, "and this is just between us, I have some financial interest in this operation. But I was shocked to hear that Etienne had involved himself, and through his girlfriend, that Annabelle person, was in trouble with Senhor Arranque and some of the other backers."

"That figures."

"My first duty is to my family. Etienne is safe now, at my own finca, under the eyes of my guards. I do not like the way this whole thing is going. What seemed to be a safe little operation at first is turning into a decidedly perilous matter. There will be a final vote this evening as to whether to continue or not. I am inclined to vote against. It will be a risky thing to do, but I have my own safeguards. You, however, are in a precarious position, Mr. Draconian."

"So I'm starting to think," Hob said.

"It's what comes of trying to play a lone hand. I suggest that you stick with me and Vana for the remainder of the evening. You will be safer that way."

"Thanks," Hob said. "But I've got a few other things to do."

"Well, try to be careful. We will all be lucky to get of out of this with whole skins."

# 5

JUANITO WAS JUST packing up to leave. "Aren't you leaving with us?" he asked Hob.

"I can't. I haven't found Nigel yet."

Juanito hesitated, trying to think how to phrase what he was going to say next. "Might it not be dangerous for you to stay on?"

Hob nodded glumly. "But it'll be just as dangerous for Nigel. Would you mind fixing me a tray with a bottle of champagne and two glasses?"

"Okay," Juanito said. He set up a good-looking tray with two chilled champagne glasses on it and a bottle of the hotel's finest champagne. "I guess you know what you're doing."

Hob didn't. But he had always suspected that the greater part of being a private detective was a willingness to fake it when you didn't know what else to do.

He left the kitchen with his tray, his bottle of champagne, his white napkin, and his two flute glasses. He knew this move wouldn't be very good for his disguise, of course, but Hob was trying to look at it positively. People who didn't know him would think he was just a waiter looking for a hotel guest, while people who did know him would think it was just Hob Draconian off on one of his weird numbers. It wasn't much, but it seemed the best he could do right now with the party closing and Nigel still not in sight. And he really did have to find Nigel.

The public portion of the party was breaking up, but there

were still a lot of guests around. He sorted through them, hoping to find Nigel before Arranque found him. He worked his way quickly through the crowd, trying to catch a glimpse of Nigel's familiar burly figure. Nigel didn't seem to be in the main lobby.

Hob spotted a flight of stairs with people all up and down it, holding drinks and chatting. He went up the stairs. At the top he came to a corridor. One way led to numbered rooms—the guests' quarters. But the other way had a discreet sign: ART GALLERY.

He went through a set of swinging doors and entered a corridor with framed paintings hung down either side. This had to be the stuff Nigel had bought on the cheap, because Hob, in all his years as a crypto-art critic, had never seen such a miserable array of paintings whose best feature was their frames. The paintings were not just bad, they were execrable; no, more than execrable. They were beneath contempt. He was looking at art so bad, it could have served as a caricature of what some people think art is all about. It would have been apt as a symbol of why fine European seventeenth- and eighteenth-century art is scoffed at in blue-collar homes all over the Western world. These paintings were to Western art as a satyr to Hyperion, to invert Shakespere's famous image; or as a hurdy-gurdy is to a Monteverdi requiem, to hazard one of his own.

Hob came to a set of doors at the far end of the corridor. He didn't like the look of those doors. Prophetic lines from *The Rubaiyat* sounded in his head:

There was a door to which I had no key
There was a something through which I could not see;
Some little talk a while of me and thee
And then no more of thee and me.

Those doors marked where the art gallery ended, and the real world presumably began again. Hob hesitated a moment and was about to turn back—a modern Eurydice giving up on Orpheus—when the doors swung open, and two men walked through.

There was rock to the right and rock to the left
And low lean thorn between
And thrice you could hear a breech-bolt snick
Where ne'er a man was seen. . . .

Funny how poetry of an ominous sort often echoed in Hob's mind at times of imminent danger. Although these men were dressed as guests, something about them—the black hair at their wrists perhaps, the livid knife scars on their cheeks, their beetled foreheads and prognathous jaws—told him they were probably hotel security.

In his best Spanish he asked them, "Excuse me, gentlemen, would you know where I might find Señor Nigel Wheaton?"

The two glanced at each other; a glance that told Hob nothing whatsoever. The larger and more mendacious looking of the two said, "Yes, señor, we were just helping him with the hanging of the pictures."

That didn't sound just right, but Hob let it pass. "A client has sent him this bottle of champagne. Do you know where I could find him?"

"Of a surety," the smaller man said. "Señor Wheaton was just picking up his check before departing. If you come with us, I think we can catch him before he leaves."

Hob followed the men through a new set of swinging doors and down the hall. In point of fact, he didn't exactly follow them. He followed the smaller man, who led, and the other man brought up the rear, thus making Hob what is technically known as the Filling in a Bozo Sandwich. A more suspicious man than Hob might have thought something was amiss. As a matter of fact, Hob thought so, too: But what the hell, in for a penny, in for a pound—and, anyway, it just might all turn out all right. He followed the men through a section of the hotel that seemed strangely deserted. They came to yet another door at the end of the hall.

"Right in through here," the smaller man said, an expression on his face that reminded Hob very much of the expression worn by the malignant cripple in Browning's "Childe Roland to the Dark

Tower Came," when he directed the knight to his peril. Still, it was no time to brood on literary apprehensions. The smaller man opened the door. Hob entered. The larger man hulked in behind him.

Inside the room, Hob came face to face with Señor Ernesto Arranque, sitting behind a large mahogany desk and looking pleased with himself.

"Come right in, Mr. Draconian," Arranque said. "We have been expecting you."

Hob glanced around to see who else had been expecting him. As he had somehow suspected, there was Nigel, slumped on the couch in a sitting position with his eyes closed, a nasty bruise high on his forehead, out cold.

Hob seemed to have missed the opening of this special party within a party. But he suspected he was in plenty of time for the main festivities.

Nigel suddenly stirred and opened his eyes. "Ah, Hob. There you are. Didn't happen to bring anyone with you, did you?"

"Like who?" Hob asked.

"Like Jean-Claude and a platoon of his tough friends. No, I can see without even asking that you didn't bring anyone. Came alone, didn't you?"

It sounded as if Nigel was chiding him.

"Well, more's the pity then," Nigel said. He looked at Arranque and said, "You fellows didn't have to crack me quite so hard." He touched the bruise on his head tenderly.

"I apologize for that," Arranque said. "Jaime is a new man. He still hasn't learned finesse."

The two men who had come in with Hob were both grinning. They didn't seem too discomfited by what Arranque was saying. Indeed, Arranque seemed to be in a high good mood, and his two helpers shared in it with him.

"I really don't see what you have against me." Nigel said. "I'll admit the paintings are not of the first water. But what do you expect at twenty pounds a throw?"

"I have no objections to the paintings," Arranque said. "My difficulty—or rather, your difficulty—lies in your association with

Mr. Draconian—something I did not know when Mr. Santos recommended you to me."

"Ah," Nigel said. "Thought it might be something like that. "You have something against Hob?"

"I'm afraid so," Arranque said. "He's been looking into a matter that I'm associated with."

"Hob," Nigel said, "have you been making waves again?"

"If investigating a murder is making waves," Hob said, "I stand guilty."

"Well, there you have it," Arranque said. "He calls it 'investigating a murder.' I call it prying into my private affairs. I'm afraid I really can't permit that. I thought I had gotten rid of Mr. Draconian in England. And now he turns up here. And now, of course, I also learn that you are his associate in this so-called detective agency of his."

"What do you mean, 'so-called'?" Hob asked. "If you wouldn't call it a detective agency, what would you call it?" He was genuinely curious.

"I know all about your association with MI16," Arranque said.

It was news to Hob. "Never heard of them," he said. "Have you, Nigel?"

Nigel shrugged, winced, and said, "Isn't that the name of a double carriageway in England? Or am I thinking of the M16?"

"This is all very droll," Arranque said. "And I suppose we could go on like this for some time. But I'm afraid there are pressing matters I must attend to. So, Mr. Wheaton, if you will excuse us, I have private matters to take up with your employer."

"Oh, certainly," Nigel said, standing up a little shakily. "I'll just slip off. Go down to the village for a beer. How would that be?"

"I'm afraid that's not what I had in mind," Arranque said. "But I appreciate your levity in this matter. The boys will escort you to where I want you to go."

The "boys" both had automatics in their hands. Hob hadn't even seen them draw them. The larger one gestured to Nigel. Nigel looked at him, looked at Hob, raised an eyebrow, and walked across the room.

"You can use the special entrance," Arranque said. He went

behind his desk and pressed a button. A panel slid open in the far wall, revealing a passageway. "Yes, this way will be better. We don't want to disturb the guests. Most of them are on their way out now, but a few remain still."

As when they had led Hob in, the smaller man took the lead. The larger man gestured at Nigel with his gun. Nigel followed the smaller man into the passageway, then turned and said to Hob, "Well, old boy, I hope you've thought of a way out of this."

"To reveal it now," Hob said, "would be premature."

The big man behind Nigel gestured with his gun again in a more preemptory manner. Nigel said, "Ta," and walked through the doorway. The large man walked in behind him. The panel slid shut.

"Well, now," Arranque said, "it's just you and me, for the moment."

"That's true," Hob said turning his attention back to Arranque. But if Hob had had any thought of leaping on him and overcoming him, he dropped it rapidly because Arranque also had a gun in his hand. It seemed as if everyone had a gun but the good guys. That wasn't the way it was supposed to be, Hob thought wistfully.

# 6

"As it turns out," Arranque said, "I am happy not to have disposed of you in England. Little did I realize at the time that I would need you for an important role here in Ibiza."

"Happy to be of service," Hob said. "What can I do for you?"

"Die for me."

"We already went through that once in England."

"Yes, but that was at the wrong time. Now we're going to do it all over again, and this time we'll do it right and at the right time. That's how the Kartel wants it."

"Which Cartel is that?" Hob asked.

"The Kali Kartel. Indian, not South American. K-A-L-I. Not C-A-L-I. And we spell Kartel with a K."

"I can see that you're having a lot of fun with these ominous forebodings," Hob said.

Just then there was a discreet rap at the door. It opened, and Silverio Vargas stepped in. He said, "Senhor Arranque, I wanted to tell you . . ." Then he saw Hob.

"Hello, friend," Hob said hopefully.

"I'm afraid not," Vargas said. "They have Etienne. Taken him from the finca." To Arranque he said, "I wanted to tell you that you could rely on my cooperation. Just don't hurt my son."

"I do not intend to," Arranque said. "As long as you continue to cooperate."

"I will do that, of course," Vargas said. He looked at Hob, hes-

itated a moment, then shrugged his shoulders and left, closing the
door softly behind him.

Hob said, "So much for the sudden rescue in the nick of time.
Could you tell me something? Why did you kill Stanley Bower?"

"It was self-protection," Arranque said. "Mr. Bower had no
right to be selling soma without an approved franchise from the
Kartel. Annabelle understood as soon as I explained it to her. Not
only was Bower selling our product illegally, he was also jump-
ing the gun, bringing soma to the market before the official grand
opening, before the regular dealers were ready to move. When I
pointed this out to him in Paris, Mr. Bower laughed at me."

"So you killed him."

"He wouldn't take me seriously. He laughed at me, Mr. Draconian. And nobody laughs at me."

Hob fought down an irresistible self-defeating impulse to
break out into giggles. Even he could see it was simply not the
time.

"So what now? When do I get out of here?"

"That will not be up to me. You can take that up with your new
hosts."

"And they are?"

"Come with me. You will meet them."

Arranque stood up and gestured with the small handgun. His
demeanor was pleasant but intent. He didn't seem to be about to
stand for any nonsense. Hob decided to go gracefully.

They went down through a side door, down a long corridor,
and into a large room with a high-domed roof. On the floor were
heavy rugs. Incense burned in braziers set into the walls. The
lighting was low and indirect, but not so indirect that Hob could
not make out a small, white-robed man at the far end of the room.
Hob was propelled forward until he stood no more than five feet
from him.

"Mr. Selim," Arranque said, "this is Hob Draconian, whom I
told you about."

"Very good, Ernesto," Selim said. "Handcuff him to that chair,
and then leave us."

Arranque did as he was told, locking Hob's left wrist to the arm of a chrome-and-leather chair. He took out another set of handcuffs to cuff the other arm, but Selim waved him off. "One will be enough. And leave the key. Thank you, Ernesto."

# 7

"OUR PRODUCT, SOMA," Selim said, "has two different aspects. As a recreational drug, the world will soon know about it. Taken by mouth it is nonaddicting—though quite habituating. It confers a sense of well-being that continues for a very long time, with a mild tail-off and no sudden drop, no 'crash' as you would say. It has none of the side effects of the better-known drugs—opium and its derivatives; cocaine and its chemical look-alike cousin, crack; methamphetamine. You do not go off into listlessness and dreamland, as on opium products, nor do you experience the irritability and tendency to paranoia that are peculiar to cocaine and its imitators."

"Sounds great," Hob said. "Maybe I'll try some sometime— when I'm in my own house, that is."

Selim smiled. "You'll try some right now, Mr. Draconian."

"No," Hob said. "Not interested."

"I haven't finished explaining the other aspect of soma. On the one hand, as I said, it is a drug with a tremendous money-making potential. A drug that the existing crime cartels—the various mafias, the Yakuza, the Triads—don't have a finger in. Mr. Arranque and his colleagues deal with that side of the matter. On the other hand, for some of us, those of the inner circle, soma is a religious rite of paramount importance and considerable antiquity."

"Is that a fact?" Hob said, because Selim had paused and seemed to be waiting for him to say something.

"Yes, it is. I do not expect the drug dealers we have assembled to take any cognizance of that aspect of it. But we of the inner council—we of the cult of Kali—consider it the most important aspect of all."

"That's very interesting," Hob said. "But what I really want to know is, what are you going to do with me?"

"I'm coming to that," Selim said. "Obviously no one wants you around for the opening of the hotel—and concurrently, the soma trade. At our request, Señor Arranque turned you over to us. We wish you to assist us in our ceremony of worship to the god Soma."

"Oh, sure," Hob said. "If you'd like me to hold a candle, or even join in the singing—I've a pretty good voice, you know— I'd be pleased to."

"We had in mind a more important position for you. Are you familiar with the Greek term *pharmakos?*"

"I don't believe I've come across that one," Hob said. "Does it mean 'guest of honor'?"

"In a way, it does. It's a Greek word, but the custom comes from India. Literally, it means, 'the sacred sacrifice.'"

Hob smiled to show he could take a joke as well as the next man. But Selim wasn't smiling. His face was grave, and the look in his eyes was compassionate.

"Believe me," Hob said, "you don't want me for your sacrificial goat. My screams will take away from the seriousness of the occasion."

"There's no thought of forcing you against your will," Selim said. "The victim has to be willing."

"Guess that rules me out," Hob said.

Selim pressed a button under his desk. The door opened and two large men entered. They went directly to Hob and held him down, one on each arm. Selim opened a table drawer and took out a gleaming hypodermic loaded with a greenish fluid.

"The usual dose is oral," Selim said. "But that's when soma is used as a recreational drug. It has a far more powerful effect when it's injected."

"No!" Hob screamed. It was a trite exclamation, but he was

rushed for time and not in an inventive mood. Selim pushed the needle into his upper arm and slowly emptied the syringe into him. Then he stepped back, and the two men released Hob's arms.

"And now," Selim said, "I think you may want a little nap. There's still time before the ceremony begins. You might even want a bit of refreshment."

"I'm not doing this willingly!" Hob shouted.

"If you really decide against it when the time comes," Selim said, "we'll try to work out something else."

Hob couldn't think of an answer to that. He felt the room beginning to spin around him. Lights flashed in his eyes, and he heard the chords of an impossibly deep-throated organ. Then he passed out.

# 8

WHEN HOB RETURNED to consciousness, he discovered that a wonderful thing had happened. He had changed into a god. It was the nicest thing he could have hoped for. Someone had taken his handcuffs off. That saved him the trouble of floating out of them. He stood up—or rather levitated to his feet. Though his body looked about the same as he remembered it, he knew it had become unbelievably powerful and supple. In the center of his being, that area the ancient Greeks had called the *thumos*, his guts had been replaced by a compact power conversion system. It was capable not only of creating unlimited energy but also of converting food into the most amazing substances.

What had that silly man, Selim, call him? The *pharmakos!* And of course that was what he was, for his *thumos*, the churning engine of his interior, was capable of synthesizing an endless range of drugs and pharmaceuticals, mood enhancers of every style and description, brain enhancers of unbelievable potency.

His attention shifted to his mind, employing the Apollonian art of self-reflection. He realized at once that while he had been sleeping, the pharmaceutical factory in his body had been busy supplying his brain-mind with everything it needed for supreme function. He was, for example, capable of instant, lightning calculation. How much was 4442.112 multiplied by 122234.12? Why, 4,005,686,002311! It was as simple as that! What was the square root of 34456664? Well, 456.22! The answers came to him immediately. He didn't even have to check them out. They were right because he was incapable of being wrong.

Along with his great intellectual and physical abilities, he had also inherited the great, never-to-be-ruffled happiness of the gods. Merely to stand here in this little room contemplating himself was joy past anything he had ever known—past what *any* mortal had ever known. And this joy was his—not for just an hour, not for just a day, not for just a year, but always. How well the old song expressed it!

He was aware that his former friend Nigel had been captured and his former acquaintance Etienne also. They were in a situation that worldly men might call dangerous. But that didn't matter. He moved around the room, taking care not to go floating off into space. A god was known by his self-restraint. And Hob was not going to jeopardize his godhead by doing anything silly.

No, he had work to do. These good people of the soma, the Kali Cult people, of whom he was the supreme example and representative, wanted him to be their *pharmakos,* their sacrifice. And how happy he was to do that, because it was, after all, a celebration of himself, and that was the nicest celebration of all.

They had paid him the supreme compliment. They wanted to sacrifice him. It was so good of them that it renewed his faith in mortals. They could call it killing, but of course a god could not die.

It was pleasant to think of these matters, but he had no time to dwell on them because already his mind was contemplating the things he would create as soon as he had the time to tend to them. Because of course he saw now that he was supremely creative. The great tapestried chords of entire symphonies crashed through his head; more than symphonies, symphony-cycles of a reach and depth that not even poor old Beethoven had been able to conceive. He saw that his talents extended to painting, as well, and that what Rembrandt had begun, he could finish; what Michaelangelo had attempted, he could accomplish; what Blake had hinted at, he could portray in full.

It was nice, it was so nice, to think of these matters, to live, in

Shelley's words, "like a poet hidden in the light of thought, singing songs unbidden til the world is wrought to sympathy with hopes and fears it heeded not." Poor, silly old Shelley! He'd make that dream come true for him, in poetry that Shakespeare would have envied. . . .

He didn't hear the door of his little room open, but when the man stood in front of him, he was not surprised to see him there because he had in fact willed that the man be there, and be there now, because there was no other time.

"Lord," the man said, "how are you feeling?"

"It is good," Hob said in deep, thrilling tones. "It is very good, Selim, my servant."

"I am so happy, master."

"I know that you are happy, Selim. And I am happy, too, because happiness for a god consists in the happiness he can bring to the lesser beings around him."

"Put that down!" Selim said sharply, and a man standing beside him pushed a gun into his pocket and fumbled for a pen. "I told you there'd be no need for weapons. Is there, Lord?"

"What need of coercion for the willing?" Hob said, smiling at his own subtlety.

"And take down that, too," Selim said. "Where is the cassette recorder? We must not lose one word of the god's utterances. Oh, my king, I am so happy to see you this way."

"There is no other way to be," Hob said gently, his smile all enveloping. "But tell me, is it not time for the ceremony?"

"Out of your own mouth you have said it, Lord! Yes, the time is close, the worshippers are making their final preparations, the altar is prepared, and the sacrifice soon may begin."

"Then leave me and finish your preparations," Hob said, thinking what an amusing memory it would be, to look back and remember how he had been killed. He couldn't remember having done that before. It was probably the last thing he needed to become a full-fledged god.

# 9

ALONE AGAIN, HOB was feeling very good, indeed. He was calm and centered, waiting for the ceremony to begin. But he was also ready for anything. A god was always ready for whatever happened. So he was not at all surprised when the door opened and in came his friend Peter Two, the dope dealer. With many a glance back over his shoulder, Peter entered and closed the door.

"Oh, Hob," Peter said. "I can't tell you how unhappy I am about this."

"What are you talking about?" Hob asked.

"The sacrifice thing. I had no idea until a few minutes ago that they were going to sacrifice you. I thought maybe they were going to do a chicken or a goat. But these people are serious. Oh, Hob, I feel so bad about this."

"What's the matter?" Hob asked. "Are they going to sacrifice you, too?"

"Oh, no," Peter said.

"Then what are you doing here?"

"I'm part of the ceremony, of course," Peter said. "In a manner of speaking, the sacrifice is to me. Not really me, but me as the stand-in for the god Soma."

"That's pretty flattering," Hob said. "How did they come to pick you for a job like that?"

"Well, you know, it's like, you know, I started this whole thing."

Hob waited.

"I invented soma, Hob. That's why I'm here now. In a manner of speaking, I'm the founding father of the present-day cult. But believe me, I had no idea it was going to come to this."

"That's interesting," Hob said. "I thought you dealt only in hashish."

"Well, I have tended to specialize in it," Peter said. "And I've prided myself on being the best hashish dealer on the island, maybe in Europe—hell, maybe in the world. No one has gone to the pains I have to ensure quality."

"I know that," Hob said. "You've always had a very high reputation. But how did you get into this soma thing?"

"It's a long story," Peter said.

"I have time," Hob said.

"I don't know how much time we have left before they want to begin. But at least I'll take a shot at it."

He settled back in one of the chairs. His low, flat, somewhat hoarse voice began to take up the tale of his association with soma.

Peter's part in this story began in Karachi, Pakistan, almost two years before Irito Mutimani's death in New York's Chinatown. Peter had left Ibiza for a business trip and gone first to India, then to Pakistan. Although his usual source of hashish was Morocco, he had grown dissatisfied with the local product. Peter was a fanatic. He sold only the best stuff, and he did the final processing himself, at his own farm near Djerba in Morocco. But he had grown unhappy with the quality of dope available that year in Morocco and throughout the Maghreb. Peter had decided, what the hell, he'd go to Pakistan where the best stuff came from.

He had gone to see Hassan, a hashish middleman of his acquaintance, at his comfortable home in the suburbs of Karachi. There were gun-toting guards outside the mud walls, giving that sense of security so important in dope transactions. Peter and Hassan sat in Hassan's walled garden, smoking the incredible double-zero hashish that only dealers get, in a water pipe the way it was meant to be. Beautiful, obsequious women brought around trays of sweetmeats, iced sherbert, and *chai*.

They discussed the increased difficulties of the dope trade. How good it used to be a few years ago. What a gentlemanly occupation. A family trade, handed down from generation to generation.

"But what will my son do?" Hassan asked. "I can't honestly recommend the trade to him. It's getting too dangerous. The way others, outsiders, are muscling in, taking over."

Peter nodded, lost in the familiar stupor of an oft-repeated conversation. He said, "You and I have a nice operation here, my friend, but it's going to hell. Getting dangerous. They're squeezing all of us out. The Triads and mafias are taking over. If only we had a nice self-contained operation. Our own thing."

Hassan sighed. "Ah, my friend, if only we had soma."

"What's that?" Peter asked.

"Soma is the ancient master drug of the Indo-European peoples. It's mentioned in the Upanishads. There was even a god of soma."

"What ever happened to the stuff?"

"It disappeared thousands of years ago. But while it was here, it was king."

Peter asked, "Has anyone tried to reproduce this soma?"

"Not to my knowledge," Hassan said

"I don't see why it couldn't be done. We know the effects we're looking for. No reason soma or something like it couldn't be redeveloped."

"Could you do it?"

Peter shrugged. "Maybe. But it would take a lot of money. I'd need to rent a lab and get a good biochemist to work with me. But given our present-day knowledge of these matters, I see no reason why it couldn't be done."

A few days later, Hassan brought Selim to meet Peter. Selim was Indian; a slim, dark-eyed man from Bombay, with a mustache that curled up at the ends. From the obsequious way that Hassan acted around him, Peter got the idea that Selim was someone of great importance.

After the usual pleasantries, Selim got to the point. "My friend Hassan tells me you think you could make soma."

"I said maybe," Peter said. "You never know about these things until you get into them. And it would cost a lot. A lab, my salary, a salary for a biochemist, other expenses."

"Suppose we could meet those expenses," Selim said. "Would you be willing to try?"

"Sure, I'd be interested. But you gotta understand, there's a big chance of failure."

"I will not worry about that," Selim said, "as long as you do your best. I can advance you the money you will need. If the enterprise turns out to be a mere chimera, an illusion, I can write it off. And there will be no hard feelings, as you Americans say."

"Would you want a contract?" Peter asked.

"No paper contract would suffice because what we are agreeing to is unenforceable. Our agreement must be verbal, and based on our understanding of what each other wants. That, in turn, must be based on knowing what you yourself want. Do you really want to make this attempt"

"I'd love to," Peter said.

"I will have to send someone to accompany you. A purely precautionary measure, you understand."

"Sure," Peter said. "Who is he?"

"It is a she," Selim said. "My daughter, Devi."

The moment Peter laid eyes on her, two months later in Ibiza, he was hopelessly hooked.

That's how the matter began. O. A. Kline's part in all this began about six months later, when Peter returned to the New York area for a brief visit.

One of the first things he did was to look up his old college chum, Otto Albert Kline, or O.A. as he prefered to be called.

They met at O.A.'s split-level home in Teaneck, New Jersey. O.A. was fattish and bespectacled. His wife, Marilyn, was a scrawny lit. major, unwillingly staying home to take care of the two children, six and seven, and teaching an English Lit. night class at the Teaneck Community College. O.A. was a bright young man. But there were many like him. He had no managerial skills. The best he'd been able to find was a dull job in an industrial lab in Tenafly, testing synthetic fiber products, a fairly simple repetitive job that an ape could perform if only it were motivated.

When Marilyn left for her consciousness-raising session, Peter got right to the point

"You ever do any more work on drugs?" he asked. There had been a time when O.A. had been a considerable underground chemist.

"No," O.A. said. "But I'd like to."

Peter described the qualities of soma as described in the literature: a godlike high with no loss of control, no physical or mental aftereffects, no habituation, energy always present in abundance, no comedown, and, best of all, no bust because the stuff would employ none of the ingredients proscribed by a killjoy society.

"Sounds great," O.A. said. "Is there any such drug?"

"Not yet. I propose that we create one."

O.A. was skeptical until Peter mentioned what he could pay: Seventy thousand a year for openers, all expenses, and a share in the profits of the new/old drug if and when it was developed.

"Sounds great," Peter said. "How many years can you guarantee at that price?"

"One," Peter said. "You get one year to come up with something. If it's anything me and my partners can use, we double your salary and the gravy train begins. If there's nothing in it—and you ought to know in a year—then you go your way and we go ours and no hard feelings."

"A year isn't much time," O.A. said. "I'd need at least six months just to set up a lab, research the literature, begin."

"Make it a year and a half," Peter suggested.

"Make it two years."

"Done," Peter said, feeling generous with Selim's money.

Next they came to the matter of setting up the lab. O.A. wanted something with a cover that would deceive or at least satisfy anyone looking into it. The best was to buy a small existing business, one that had recently gone belly-up and could be purchased for a song. Marilyn had to be consulted. The story they told her was that O.A. was going to look into the duplication of an existing process, a food additive unprotected by patent. If he could successfully duplicate the process, it could be sold to a Swiss firm that was paying through the nose for the original product. Marilyn thought it all sounded a little bogus but didn't seem to be dangerous in a legal sense. And the money sounded good. That much income would let her quit her teaching job and devote full time to completing her long-delayed novel about growing up the only Jewish girl of Chinese parentage in a small South Carolina town.

"So how's it going?" Peter Two asked five months later. He had returned from Ibiza to see how O.A. was getting on. O.A. had a harried look. His eyes were red-rimmed. He exhibited various signs of nervousness, including rubbing one finger against another.

"I think I'm onto something," O.A. said. "The most recent batch is quite promising."

"You don't look so good," Peter said. "Are you also *on* something?"

O.A. gave a ragged laugh. "On something? What do you think? Somebody has to test this stuff to see where we're getting. I can't ask Marilyn to do it. I can't try it out on the kids. I can't put an ad in the paper asking for volunteers for a groovy new drug in the developmental stage. I have to try the stuff out on myself."

"You're sounding a little strange," Peter observed.

"Of course I am," O.A. said. "What do you expect? I won't have soma until I have it, will I? And meantime I have to test all the stuff that doesn't work, or that works but has drawbacks—like giving blinding headaches or setting the pulse up to dancing rhythm, or turning the extermities to ice, or any of the other thousands of things I've found."

"This is not a good situation," Peter said, observing that O.A. seemed to be ranging up toward hysteria when he was not drifting down toward stupor. "This is going to play hell with your concentration."

"You're telling me?" O.A. said, his voice rising above the loud hum of conversation in the coffee shop.

"Tell you what," Peter said. "Cool out for a while. I'm going to find you someone to guinea pig for you."

"Is that safe?"

"A lot safer than what you're doing now."

Peter was as good as his word. Later that day he returned to O.A.'s apartment. With him he brought a young, short, stocky man, Japanese by the look of him, with bristly close-cropped black hair and an open and frank expression.

"This is Irito Mutinami. Irito's an old friend from Ibiza."

The two men shook hands. Irito said, "I was there in '60 and '61. Greatest place on earth. The babes. And the drugs. Man, it was too much. When were you there?"

"Just one summer in '74," O.A. said.

One summer wasn't much, but it was enough for membership in the club of Ibizaphiles. The two men exchanged the names of people they both knew. They reminisced about beaches they had lain on, restaurants they had eaten in, girls they had known in common, and other details of the bonding code of exiles. Soon they were perfectly satisfied with each other.

"I laid out the position for Irito," Peter said. "He'll be happy to test your drugs for you. He lives in Chinatown, so he'll be handy to come over and ingest whatever your latest concoction is. I'm taking care of his pay."

"Fine, fine." O.A. felt he had to add, "I hope you know what you're getting into, Irito."

"Call me Tom. That's what they call me at home. Hey, guys, this is great. I mean, imagine being paid to test groovy drugs! I mean, it's the sort of thing I'd pay *you* for if I was heeled. It's like a dream. What did Khayyam say? 'I often wonder what the vintners buy one half so precious as the goods they sell.' I mean, it's that kind of a situation."

"You're Japanese?" O.A. asked.

"Third generation."

"If you don't mind my asking, what are you doing living in Chinatown?"

"I lucked into a one-room place on Catherine Street. Man, I got the greatest food on all sides of me. It's like a dream."

"You don't get any trouble?"

Irito, or Tom, shrugged. "Why should I get any trouble? I'm just another foreigner to them."

"Can you start this afternoon?" O.A. asked.

"Hey, man, I can start right now."

"This may not be quite as groovy as you expect, Tom."

"No problem. I can handle bummers."

"I'll be on my way," Peter said, rising. "I think we've solved a problem here, O.A. I'll be in touch."

Peter left. O.A. went to the lab's inner room and came back with a test tube half full of a viscous blue substance.

"What do you call this?" Irito asked, lifting the tube.

"No name yet. This is just Run Three forty-two A."

"Nice name," Irito said. "I like it already."

And so it went. Life went better for O.A. now that he had Irito as a tester. Irito was what they used to call a dead-game dopehead. When he got high, he liked it. When he was brought down, it amused him. The only stipulation that O.A. made was that Irito not take any other narcotic or alcoholic substance during the period of testing. It would only confuse the results of the soma program. Irito was a little reluctant to give up his marijuana. It was helping him get through his accountancy course at NYU. But he promised, and he was a boy-man of his word. As it turned out, he didn't miss marijuana at all. O.A.'s continuing work gave him many different head trips to contemplate, some of them pleasant, all of them interesting.

# 10

HOB LOVED HIS sacrifice outfit. They gave it to him soon after
Peter left swearing he'd do what he could, but he didn't see what
he could do. Hob's followers brought him clean trousers, a shirt,
and a three-quarter-length jacket, all of finest Japanese crepe.
After he was dressed, they splattered him with red sandalwood
and vermillion, and then they put marigold garlands around his
neck.

So interested had Hob been in Peter's story that he had quite
forgotten that he had a task to perform. But even a god can be absentminded. In fact, who had a better right? But he remembered
when Selim returned.

The small, dapper Indian had changed into long robes and a
turban. He had brought two turbaned followers with him. They
led Hob to a little anteroom, told him they'd be back for him
soon, bowed deeply, and left him alone, closing the door softly
behind them.

Hob saw there was an open window. He went to it and took
a deep breath. Below was a gently sloping roof. It would be so
easy to go out across the roof, down the drainpipe, out to the
green wooded land below. They had been so attentive to everything else, but they had overlooked this. So it went in the affairs
of men. Humans tried to take care of every possibility but always
left something undone. He looked out the window, then closed
and locked it. He, the god, escape? He wouldn't miss what was
coming next for anything in the world.

He sat for a while in perfect one-pointed meditation. He was ready when they came for him.

Hob knew it was time for the ceremony, and he was eager for it to begin. He had that old-time religious feeling. You don't see a lot of that anymore: the willing sacrifice.

Taking care to keep his feet on the ground and not float above their heads as he could so easily have done, Hob walked with Selim and the several others out of the anteroom, down a corridor, through a doorway, down another corridor, and so on, until he came to a big room, an auditorium sort of room. It was filled with worshipers, all of them men. On one side, about half of them were Indian, wearing white robes and white turbans. Across the aisle, the others were in business dress. The two groups sat in rows of folding chairs on different sides of the room, like friends of the bride and friends of the groom.

There was a scattering of applause as Hob walked down the aisle. Hob nodded to them as he walked out onto the little stage in the front of the room. He nodded in a most friendly, if condescending, manner—for he had already determined he would not be an austere, standoffish god, but rather a familiar, friendly one, a god anyone could talk to, one willing to do anything for his people. Selim was just behind him, at his right elbow, as was proper for the leader of his cult.

Selim began intoning a chant, and the other turbaned people took it up, a deep-voiced chant, antiphonal, with breaks in the recital in which Hob himself spoke forth, his voice brazen and splendid, saying the unknown words of a new language that he would teach them later, when he had been reborn.

To one side of the stage was a long, low, marble altar with a pure-white fleece thrown over it and lying on that, the long black-bladed knife with which the ceremony would be performed. An overhead spotlight bathed it in white radiance. Hob knew that the altar was where he was supposed to be. He walked up to it and a hush came over the worshipers. Examining it, he saw that the marble was carved deeply and looked very old. The carving showed two figures on either side of what looked like a tree of life. The figures were raised from the stone, standing out in high relief, whereas the tree was incised deep into the rock. It took Hob a moment to figure out why this was so. Then he realized that the deeply chiseled tree would carry away his blood when he was sacrificed. He was pleased to see a suitable receptacle of onyx situated beneath the blood channel. Not a drop of his blood would be lost.

He was joined now by young acolytes wearing smart-looking crimson cloaks with hoods, swinging censers in which incense was burning. Frankincense and myrrh—how appropriate. It had never been like this back when Hob had attended synagogue. Perfumed smoke twisted its way toward the ceiling.

The place was dark; no, not exactly dark but dim. As Hob's eyes grow accustomed to the gloom he saw, standing behind the chanting acolytes, a whole bunch of hybrid animals: lions combined with zebras, rhinoceroses whose lower parts were snakes. What did they call them? Chimeras! The chimeras were symbolic beasts, and modern rationalism said they never existed. How wrong they were! He was looking at them now!

His all-knowledge informed him that for many centuries, several orders of creation had interacted on the earth, not just men and animals, but chimeras also and, of course, spirits and gods. It made Hob feel good to realize that his own willing compliance in this ceremony of death was playing its part in calling forth the ancient gods to live again.

And the scene kept on changing, which was charming but a little bewildering. Now it was like a landscape by Dalí, now a landscape filled with architecture by Gaudí. To one side Hob saw an open coffin. It was empty. He was puzzled by it for a moment, then realized it was meant for him. It was where they would put his body after they sacrificed him. His body, but not him, for he, of course, could not die; he would simply create a new body as soon as he'd discarded the old one.

Looking around the room again, he saw other things that perplexed him for a moment and would have made him think he was hallucinating if he hadn't known better. Something floppy was making its way across the room. A walking catfish! And there was a two-headed calf, one head bawling for its mother, the other head blinking incuriously at the plump hermaphrodite leading it.

All in all, it was just the sort of thing that could have been staged on the shores of the Ganges. And that was deeply satisfying.

There was someone coming toward him wearing an elaborate gold headgear.

"Are you ready?" he asked Hob. It was Selim.

"Ready as I'll ever be," Hob said lightly. He knew he ought to be taking this more seriously, but it was difficult, he was just feeling too good, everything was too funny. He only hoped he didn't ruin their ceremony with his Zarathustrian levity.

Then people were urging him gently toward the altar. At last, it was time! When he was standing in front of it, they pressed their hands on his shoulders. Silly of them. All they had to do was tell him to kneel. He did so, and put his head where they indicated. Now all was in readiness. He could see how they had it planned out. Hob merely had to tilt back his head and someone would cut his throat with that long, sharp, wavy knife. Like slicing a pot roast, Hob thought, and had to suppress his laughter.

Now the music was coming up. Funny, he hadn't seen any orchestra. Perhaps they were concealed behind the walls. They were tootling and banging away now, an oriental clangor. Or maybe it was a recording. The chanting went on over the orchestra and quickly mounted in intensity. Hob couldn't make out the tune.

Then a priestess came forward and picked up the black-bladed knife. She was masked as a bird, some kind of hawk. She was wearing a jeweled halter and gauze pants gathered at the ankles. Quite an attractive body, very white under the overhead lights, vaguely familiar. When Hob reached up and gently removed her mask, he was not too surprised to find Annabelle under it.

# 11

"I TOLD YOU I had something really big going for me," Annabelle said. The mask had smeared her makeup, but she still looked fine.

"I had no idea you meant this," Hob replied. He was still smiling, but not feeling quite as good as he had before. In fact, he was starting to feel a little weird.

"I'm sorry it has to be you," Annabelle said. "But objectively, as a friend, maybe you can feel good for me. Being high priestess of the newest cult in the world is something, isn't it?"

"Your parents would be proud of you," Hob said. And then he heard someone's voice from the audience, saying, loud and clear, "This isn't fair! I won't stand for it!"

And then a woman came marching out of the audience and up to the stage beside Hob and Annabelle. She looked familiar, too.

It was Devi, wearing a long white robe, her face set and furious. Peter, looking unhappy and embarrassed, was just getting to the stage beside her.

"Devi, please," Peter said.

"You son of a bitch," Devi said to him. "You promised me I could be the high priestess. What's this English bitch doing here?"

"Now, wait a minute, sister," Annabelle said. "I was promised this by the top man, Señor Arranque. I made all this possible."

"You didn't do diddly squat," Devi said, revealing a grasp of English made complete through Stephen King novels. "And who is this Arranque? Just a common criminal! I am the daughter of

Selim, the head of the cult, and I am married to the creator of soma!"

"Now just everybody hold on just a moment!" Hob said in his best Jimmy Stewart imitation. "I think I've got something to say about this!"

There were cries from the audience: "Let the sacrifice speak!"

"Let's hear what the *Pharmakos* has to say!"

And just a moment after that, all hell broke loose as a door in the back opened, and in walked a tall Englishman and a taller black man.

# 12

A MURMUR OF discontent and disapprobation passed through the ranks of the attendees. Those on the left side of the auditorium were representatives of the original Kali Cult. There were about seventy of them, and they all came from the Indian subcontinent. For many of them, it was their first time away from Mother India. Europe seemed to them a strange and godless place, and Ibiza, heart of the sybaritic Mediterranean culture, was most godless of all. They were serious men, for the most part ultrareligious Brahmins, Hindustan patriots unsatisfied with India's relatively insignifant showing on the international scene and particularly disturbed by the domination of Indian crime by powerful groups from other countries. They had let Selim lead them into this new enterprise, one that would be Indian dominated, the first Hindustan mafia since the beginning of the world.

Selim had made this possible by producing, through Peter, a singular product: Soma, the epitome of drugs. But he had also had to compromise. To get soma onto the international scene and not leave it a merely local product—as qat was in Yemen or unprocessed coca leaves in Peru and Bolivia—he had had to form a partnership with foreign criminal elements.

It was members of this other criminal element, sitting on the right side of the auditorium, who were in equal attendance here at the rites of Kali.

There were some fifty-seven of them, criminals from all over Europe, the Americas, and Asia, sick of their subordination to the established drug cartels of their own countries, ready to form an alliance with the Indians, with their new product, ready to supply and sell the new drug wherever it might be wanted.

There was no love lost between these two groups.

The Indians considered the Europeans scum of the earth, riffraff who hadn't succeeded in their native lands.

The Europeans considered the Indians tradition-bound fuddy-duddies who had lucked onto a product and expected to use the enterprise and expertise of others to bring them wealth.

The animosity between the two groups was already high. It was brought to the point of explosion by the sight of two women—one European, one Asiatic—struggling on a stage for a black-handled knife.

The final element in the impending explosion of the spark came when the two men suddenly entered the auditorium, the tall, ruddy Englishman with tawny hair and a leonine face and the tall black warrior from Brazil.

And to make it all the more enigmatic, the Englishman was singing. It was a song that none in that audience knew. The only man present who seemed to know it was Hob Draconian, the sacrifice, and it galvanized him into belated action.

Hob's mind had cleared sufficiently for him to recognize that the bearded Englishman was Nigel, and the tall, thin black man accompanying him was Etienne. But why was Nigel singing, and, more important, what was the song?

He could just make out the words above the increasing hubbub of the assembly—even the two battling women parted a moment to listen—something about an Englishman's home being his castle . . .

A song whose melody was hauntingly familiar, bringing up, as it did, images of khaki-clad heroism against loinclothed and turbaned hordes of fanatics in an underground place lit only by flaring torches . . .

Of course! It was Cary Grant's song, "An Englishman's Home is His Castle," that he had sung in the movie *Gunga Din,* in the part where, trapped in the underground chambers of the Kali cult's headquarters, he had distracted the hordes of Kali worshipers long enough for Gunga Din to escape and warn the colonel and have him bring the regiment. . . .

But why was Nigel acting so crazy? And Etienne, too! It didn't occur to Hob that they might also have been sampling the soma.

"Nigel!" Hob called.

"Hang on, old boy!" Nigel called back. "Help is on its way."

"The colonel? The regiment?"

"Lieutenant Navarro and his trusty Guardia Civil. They'll have to do."

Now Arranque sprang to his feet from his seat among the Europeans. "Kill that man!" he cried, pointing to Hob.

"But he is the sacrifice," Selim said, also standing up from his seat among the Hindus. "No one must touch him except the high priestess."

"I'm the high priestess!" cried Devi, snatching the knife from Annabelle's hand.

"The hell you say, bitch!" Annabelle screamed, snatching back the knife.

"My daughter is supposed to be the high priestess!" Selim thundered.

"No, my people put up the money, and that job is for my girl-friend!" Arranque thundered back.

There was a frozen moment, a bit of stop action that Hob, though he was coming down from his high, was nevertheless able to appreciate.

In that big auditorium room, with the overhead lights flick-ering like witches' fires; with Annabelle and Devi at each other's throats; with Nigel and Etienne, frozen snarls on their faces, fac-ing the multitude; with Hob ripping off his mask and returning to a mood of self-preservation; with Arranque and Slim glaring at each other like caged jaguars in a jungle setting with a huge yel-low moon rising and tribal drums beating in the background; with the guests, both Indian-traditional and international-modern, reaching for the guns concealed in their inner jacket pockets—at that moment, with the whole shooting works poised to go off like a keg of gunpowder falling into a volcano, it required only one thing to set it all off.

Silverio Vargas, perhaps inadvertently, supplied that one thing. Rising from his chair, with Vana beside him, he shouted, "Etienne! Come to me! I will get you out of this!"

The fact that he spoke in Portuguese made no difference at all. Everyone, at that superheated moment, knew very well what he meant.

It was every man for himself time, and the devil or Kali or whatever infernal diety that was presiding take the hindermost.

And suddenly the air was full of bullets.

They were bullets of all calibers, from deadly little .22s zinging around like steel-winged hummingbirds, to the middle calibers—stern, businesslike .32s and .38s, winging on their errands of destruction with precision and even a certain dignity—while the big fellows, the stately 9mms and the big-shouldered .357s, as well as the almost legendary .44s and the .45s, crashed around that room like castanets of death played by Red Murder and his Gunpowder Band. These bullets, large and small, ricocheted off wall and floor, took out lighting fixtures and vases full of imported flowers, and smashed into the flesh of many a cowering manthing with attendant gushes of blood. And they were no respecter of race or creed, these bullets, as they blundered around the auditorium on their impersonal mission of death. Bullets smashed into chairs behind which many of the combatants, like the Mexican bandits in the climatic scene of Sam Peckinpah's *The Wild Bunch,* crouched down to groan and curse and reload and fire again.

And just as this scene was reaching its unimaginable climax, there came a sound louder than all the rest, catching the attention of all those frenzied fighters and causing them to look around to see where it was coming from. This at a moment when bodies were falling like flies after the mother of all fulminations, and curses—some guttural, some sibilant—could be heard in half the languages of the world.

The sound came from behind the locked double doors of that ill-omened auditorium room.

Somebody was trying to break in.

There was a fascinated silence while all watched as the doors bulged under repeated heavy blows. Hob, for his part, in the first stages of his come-down, thought it was very like the final scene in Lord Dunsany's "The Idol's Eye," when the great barbaric stone statue from whom the thieves have plucked its jewel of an eye is returning, insensate animation bent on destruction.

Literary allusions were lost on the others, however. They watched, panting, some of them bleeding, as the doors shook and finally burst open.

And in marched Lieutenant Ramon Navarro with a half dozen of his trusty Guardias, just as Nigel had predicted.

There was a sudden, tomblike silence. Then Navarro said, in a loud voice that was hard as iron, "As representative of the Spanish government and its self-defense forces, and the highest ranking Guardia Civil officer on this island, Colonel Sanchez having gone off to Madrid for urgent consultations, I hereby declare that the Spanish government takes no official position at this time on the doings of foreign nationals on property owned by said nationals. However, we are extending to any Spanish nationals or Ibiza residents the right to leave this property immediately while the owners settle their own affairs."

There was a scramble as five or six Spanish waiters, who had been caught in the crossfire, moved over to the Guardia's side. Nigel moved there, too, and, after a moment, so did Hob, who had sobered up enough to opt for survival. Etienne wavered for a moment, then crossed the room to the Guardias, calling out, "Father, please join us!"

"No!" Vargas grated. "I will see this thing out!"

Peter came over and joined the Guardia ranks. "Devi?" he called out.

"I'm staying," Devi said in a voice of iron. "I'm the real priestess."

Annabelle looked defiant for a moment, then crossed over and joined the group around Navarro. "Well, if you're the priestess, I guess I'm not."

"Baby!" Arranque called. "Where are you going?"

"Sorry, Ernesto," Annabelle said. "I thought this was my big shot, but it turns out to be just one more fiasco. Just my luck, huh?"

"I will make you high priestess!" Arranque raved.

"Thanks, but no thanks. I can't afford to get killed here. I got a kid in private school in Switzerland."

The group backed out of the assembly hall under the watchful submachine guns of the Guardia. They went through the hotel lobby, which was now silent and deserted, and out through the big glass doors. As they came to the outside drive and reached the Guardia's Land Rover, Nigel stopped, frowned, turned, and began to walk back in. Hob grabbed him by the sleeve and restrained him.

"What do you think you're doing?"

"I have to go back in there," Nigel said. "I left something."

"What did you leave?"

"My mother's birthday present. A very nice silver service. It's in the main cloakroom."

Just then the crash of gunfire sounded up again.

Nigel listened for a moment, then shrugged. "Well, it was valuable—but not, I suppose, irreplacable."

# 13

THERE WAS AN aimless moment after the relatively good guys were out of the hotel. Hob asked Navarro, "What now?"

Navarro shrugged. "I have exceeded my authority. But not, I think, the proprieties of the situation."

"You mean we're free to go?" Hob asked.

"To the devil, if you wish," Navarro said. "This is what comes of letting foreigners own property in the motherland."

"In that case," Nigel said, "what about we all get a drink?"

"Not for me," Navarro said. "I have much paperwork to fill out. But perhaps lunch tomorrow?"

"We'll go to Sa Punta," Nigel said, naming the best restaurant in Santa Eulalia. "I'm paying."

"I should hope so," Navarro said and stalked off to a waiting police vehicle.

"Well, old boy, what do you say to that drink?" Nigel asked.

"El Caballo Negro ought to be open," Hob said. "Do you think a Bloody Mary will take the taste of soma out of my mouth?"

"Eventually," Nigel said.

They got into one of the taxis that, like black-and-white vultures, gathered for any event that promised to offer fares, alive or dead, and rode in companionable silence to Santa Eulalia and the cheerful sounds of El Caballo Negro.

"Well, old boy," Nigel said, two drinks later, "it has not worked out too badly, I think."

"For you," Hob said. "You must have made a nice profit from Arranque."

Nigel made a dismissive gesture. "That is beside the point. I refer to the work I brought in to the Agency."

"What work would that be?" Hob asked.

"My dear fellow! Hasn't Jean-Claude filled you in?"

"Just a lot of cryptic nonsense," Hob said.

"We, the Agency that is, are sole agents for the sale of a rather large shipment of San Isidro's art treasures."

"Was that what Santos wanted to set up?"

"Of course. The Arranque thing was just a little something on the side, as it were."

Hob stared at him, filled with a wild surmise in which, faintly, he could just glimpse the wavy outlines of money. Just then Sandy, the proprietor, came over, a slip of paper in his hand.

"This telegram came for you yesterday, Hob. Or maybe it was the day before."

Hob took it and read: SHIPMENT NOW UNLOADED AT CHERBOURG. NO PROBLEMS SO FAR. AWAITING YOUR INSTRUCTIONS. It was from Jean-Claude.

"I think there are some details you need to fill in," Hob said.

"Of course. But don't you think we had better make our travel arrangements? We don't want to leave a ten-to-twenty-million-pound cargo rotting in a warehouse in Cherbourg for too long."

"Twenty million pounds?"

"Perhaps that's an exaggeration. But the stuff should fetch a pretty price in Paris and Brussels. And ten percent of it is ours. But I still have to get my mother a birthday present."

Jean-Claude's telegram took the taste of soma completely out of Hob's mouth, replacing it with the sweet tang of anticipated money.

# 14

HOB DIDN'T MENTION the San Isidran shipment when he lunched with Fauchon a month later in Paris. He told him all the rest, however.

"And that's how it ended?" Fauchon asked, as he and Hob sat at a small outside table in Paris, at Deux Magots.

"Well, not exactly," Hob said. "Dramatically speaking, you could say Navarro's rescue of us was the climax. But there was quite a bit of falling action after that."

"I'm surprised at your friend Navarro," Fauchon said. "Surely he was taking a lot on himself."

"*Au contraire,*" Hob said. "He was merely following the orders of his superior, Colonel Sanchez. Sanchez was, and still is, the ranking Guardia Civil officer on the island. Sanchez had also been well and thoroughly bribed by the various criminal parties in this. To arrest the soma people at the hotel would have brought out his own well-paid part in the affair. The officials in Madrid, even though their part of the bribe had been passed on, would've had no recourse but to hang him out to dry."

" 'Hang him out to dry,' " Fauchon mused. "Is that an American expression?"

"Yes, it is," Hob said. "I just made it up at this moment."

"And Colonel Sanchez was in Madrid at this time?"

"No," Hob said. "He was at the Guardia Civil barracks. But when he heard what was going on, he told Ramon to say that he was off the island and to contain the situation the best way he knew how."

Fauchon shook his head. "It wouldn't have happened that way in France."

"Of course it would," Hob said. "The French police have the same tendencies as the Spanish. Either to overlook something entirely or to jump in and take too much action, thus creating a worse mess."

"Perhaps you're right," Fauchon said. "It's not like that in America?"

"I suspect it's like that everywhere," Hob said.

"So how was the matter finally resolved?"

"In the usual way. Half a dozen or so people were killed in the shoot-out at the hotel. Another dozen or so wounded. The rest patched up their differences. This was made easier now by the fact that Annabelle had withdrawn her claim as high priestess."

"And Arranque? And Silverio Vargas?"

"You'll be happy to know they both survived."

"And Etienne?"

"Alive and well. He suffered a superficial wound that allows him to carry his arm in a black silk sling. It looks very well on him."

"What was Etienne doing in the hotel in the first place? I'm not quite clear on that."

"Arranque's men had captured him from Vargas's finca and taken him to the hotel to ensure Vargas's compliance. Etienne overpowered his guard—did I mention that he was a black belt in karate?—and managed to free Nigel, too."

"I see," Fauchon said. "Did father and son manage to patch it up?"

"I believe so," Hob said. "I wasn't privy to that scene."

"And what about Annabelle? Did she make up with Arranque or return to Etienne?"

"Neither. She went to Hollywood. We still haven't heard if she was able to sell her story yet. She has an agent, however."

"And what about Stanley Bower's murderer?" Fauchon asked.

"That was Arranque," Hob said. "Not that you'll ever be able to pin it on him. That's how it goes in real life, Inspector."

"His brother will be disappointed, I suppose."

"I wrote Timothy with the information, as he requested. I haven't heard from him."

"Presumably he's satisfied," Fauchon said.

"Presumably."

"And the soma you found in the cellar?"

"The Guardia didn't want to know about it. As far as I know, it's on the streets of big cities in America and Europe. And selling briskly, I hear. But you'd know more about that than I do."

"Indeed I do," Fauchon said. "Your statement is correct, as far as it goes. Soma is indeed being sold. But the previously established criminal organizations—the Yakuza, Mafia, Triad, and so forth—have objected in no uncertain terms to this traffic, since it cuts them out. In America there's open warfare between the two organizations, the Cali Cartel and the Kali Kartel. One or the other of them is going to have to find another name. It's very like Chicago of the old days. Dealers are dying like flies. Frankly, it saves us a lot of work."

"I'm glad to hear that," Hob said. "This has not been my sort of affair at all. I'm happy to be out of it."

"Well you might be," Fauchon said.

"Anything else in mind?"

"Not at the moment. I've come into a bit of money from an uncle in Florida and so I'm fixing up my finca."

Fauchon nodded. "I think that takes care of everything. Except Nigel, of course. Did he ever get his mother's birthday present back?"

"We picked up something else for her in the Rastro in Barcelona," Hob said. "An even nicer silver service. From what Nigel told me, she was well satisfied."

"Well, that is fine," Fauchon said. "What are your plans now?"

"I'm going back to Ibiza," Hob said. "It's just coming on autumn, the best time of year there. The tourists are going home. One has time to think."

"Autumn is the best time everywhere," Fauchon said. "Pity it can't be extended year around."

## READING LOG

| | | |
|---|---|---|
| 103 | | |
| | | |
| | | |
| | | |
| | | |
| | | |
| | | |